The Three Assassins . . .

"Let's go," Longarm said, hand near his belt buckle and not far from the butt of his Colt, which rested on his left hip.

They started down the creaking stairs and when they reached the foyer, Longarm went for the door leading outside. Suddenly, he heard the faint and all too familiar squeak of Agnes's door hinges. Longarm, expecting the old woman to poke her nose out and offer a cryptic comment, turned and caught the sight of a boot and big hand an instant before the door was thrown wide open.

Tex had his gun in his fist as Longarm threw himself at the door, catching a bullet across his forearm. The force of the collision slammed the door into the three waiting gunmen. Tex was knocked off balance and Longarm was falling as Rose yanked her pistol out and fired through the half-opened door.

A man screamed and Longarm rolled, grabbing his gun and shooting blindly upward. There was a second cry of pain and then a tall, slender man with a fancy gun in his fist took an unsteady step forward, turning his aim at Rose . . .

DON'T MISS THESE
ALL-ACTION WESTERN SERIES
FROM THE BERKLEY PUBLISHING GROUP

THE GUNSMITH by J. R. Roberts

Clint Adams was a legend among lawmen, outlaws, and ladies. They called him . . . the Gunsmith.

LONGARM by Tabor Evans

The popular long-running series about Deputy U.S. Marshal Custis Long—his life, his loves, his fight for justice.

SLOCUM by Jake Logan

Today's longest-running action Western. John Slocum rides a deadly trail of hot blood and cold steel.

BUSHWHACKERS by B. J. Lanagan

An action-packed series by the creators of Longarm! The rousing adventures of the most brutal gang of cutthroats ever assembled—Quantrill's Raiders.

DIAMONDBACK by Guy Brewer

Dex Yancey is Diamondback, a Southern gentleman turned con man when his brother cheats him out of the family fortune. Ladies love him. Gamblers hate him. But nobody pulls one over on Dex . . .

WILDGUN by Jack Hanson

The blazing adventures of mountain man Will Barlow—from the creators of Longarm!

TEXAS TRACKER by Tom Calhoun

J.T. Law: the most relentless—and dangerous—manhunter in all Texas. Where sheriffs and posses fail, he's the best man to bring in the most vicious outlaws—for a price.

→•→ **TABOR EVANS** →•←

LONGARM

AND THE
SANTA FE WIDOW

JOVE BOOKS, NEW YORK

THE BERKLEY PUBLISHING GROUP
Published by the Penguin Group
Penguin Group (USA) Inc.
375 Hudson Street, New York, New York 10014, USA
Penguin Group (Canada), 90 Eglinton Avenue East, Suite 700, Toronto, Ontario M4P 2Y3, Canada
(a division of Pearson Penguin Canada Inc.)
Penguin Books Ltd., 80 Strand, London WC2R 0RL, England
Penguin Group Ireland, 25 St. Stephen's Green, Dublin 2, Ireland (a division of Penguin Books Ltd.)
Penguin Group (Australia), 250 Camberwell Road, Camberwell, Victoria 3124, Australia
(a division of Pearson Australia Group Pty. Ltd.)
Penguin Books India Pvt. Ltd., 11 Community Centre, Panchsheel Park, New Delhi—110 017, India
Penguin Group (NZ), 67 Apollo Drive, Rosedale, Auckland 0632, New Zealand
(a division of Pearson New Zealand Ltd.)
Penguin Books (South Africa) (Pty.) Ltd., 24 Sturdee Avenue, Rosebank, Johannesburg 2196,
South Africa

Penguin Books Ltd., Registered Offices: 80 Strand, London WC2R 0RL, England

This is a work of fiction. Names, characters, places, and incidents either are the product of the author's imagination or are used fictitiously, and any resemblance to actual persons, living or dead, business establishments, events, or locales is entirely coincidental.

LONGARM AND THE SANTA FE WIDOW

A Jove Book / published by arrangement with the author

PRINTING HISTORY
Jove edition / October 2011

ISBN: 978-0-515-15000-1

JOVE®
Jove Books are published by The Berkley Publishing Group,
a division of Penguin Group (USA) Inc.,
375 Hudson Street, New York, New York 10014.
JOVE® is a registered trademark of Penguin Group (USA) Inc.
The "J" design is a trademark of Penguin Group (USA) Inc.

PRINTED IN THE UNITED STATES OF AMERICA

10 9 8 7 6 5 4 3 2 1

Chapter 1

Deputy United States Marshal Custis Long was taking his leisure on a lazy Sunday afternoon in one of his favorite Denver saloons, called the Salty Dog. Flies buzzed overhead while men talked quietly and complained about the extreme heat that had gripped their mile-high city. They were saying that it would top one hundred degrees for the third straight day and that if the drought continued, the city was going to have to start rationing out water.

Longarm tilted his flat-brimmed hat back and wiped his sweaty brow. He hated this terrible midsummer heat, especially when there wasn't even a breeze to give a man a bit of comfort. He'd slept poorly the night before, and he was wondering if he could talk his boss, Marshal Billy Vail, into sending him high up into the Rockies where it was easier on a man.

Yep, he'd ask Billy first thing tomorrow morning at the office, but in the meanwhile the best he could do was to sip cool beer while reading a newspaper account of how the Republican National Convention had nominated James A.

Garfield of Ohio for President with Chester A. Arthur of
New York as his running mate. The Democratic National
Convention had nominated an old veteran, General Winfield S. Hancock of Pennsylvania. The general had fought
in both the Mexican and Civil wars, but from what Longarm could read about him, Winfield didn't seem to have
much to say of substance and mostly talked about horses,
cannons, and long-past battles.

In truth, Longarm really didn't care who won the presi-
dency as he had never been very interested in politics. So
he turned his attention to an article that noted the United
States Census Department said that there were a little over
fifty million people in the country and that the center of
the population had moved westward to Cincinnati, Ohio;
the state of New York was the largest, with a population of
just over five million.

"Too many damn people," Longarm muttered while
sipping his beer and waving the newspaper in front of his
perspiring face to cool himself and keep the flies at a distance. "*Fifty million!* Can you imagine?"

"Huh?" a man who had been napping at a nearby table
asked, raising his head off the wood and then loudly
belching.

"Dudley, this newspaper says that there are over fifty
million Americans."

"Shit," the man said, looking sadly at his empty beer
glass and giving Longarm a hopeful smile. "Who gives a
damn? All I know is that I only have five cents left in my
pocket and that won't even buy me a refill. I sure am hot
and thirsty, Custis."

Longarm drained his glass of beer and signaled for the
bartender to bring two refills. When they arrived, he and

poor Dudley raised their glasses in a halfhearted salute and drank. Longarm's eyes scanned the rest of the paper and noted with some interest that the world heavyweight bare-knuckle boxing title had been won by Paddy Ryan, who pounded the defender, Joe Goss of England, into a bloody pulp over eighty-seven brutal rounds. Goss, the lighter man, had tried to gouge out Ryan's eyeballs, but Ryan had ended the fight by bashing the lighter man's throat until he could not get sufficient air. Fouls were of course called by both sides, but most agreed that Ryan was a clear winner.

"Say, Custis?" Dudley asked.

"Yeah?"

"You wouldn't happen to have an extra cigar, would you?"

"Nope."

The man sighed and laid his head back down on the table after upending his glass. He farted, belched again, and fell fast asleep.

Longarm folded the newspaper he'd borrowed from the bar and finished his beer. He wasn't sure what he would do the rest of the swelteringly hot afternoon, but he thought he might find a shady tree in the park along Cherry Creek and take a long nap. In the evening, he would drop in to visit a fetching young woman named Miss Lucy Crabtree and see if either of them had the energy to hop in her bed and then to later venture out on the town for supper.

Longarm pushed himself to his feet and found that he was a bit unsteady. How many beers had he drunk while trying to endure this suffocating heat? Three or four, he supposed. In cold weather that wouldn't bother a man, but in this awful heat . . . well, the beer seemed more power-ful than usual.

"Here's your paper back, Sam," he said as he headed toward the swinging batwing doors.

"Say, Custis. Did you read about that heavyweight match where Paddy Ryan whipped that Englishman in eighty-seven dirty rounds?"

"Yeah."

"You ever fight professionally?" Sam asked. "I've seen you in action a few times here and you're pretty damn good with your fists."

"Oh," Longarm said modestly, "I'm not bad, but I'd never be able to make eighty-seven rounds."

"Perhaps not, but we have to remember that most of those rounds only last a few seconds, until one man throws the other to the canvas," Sam informed him. "Best fights are always those that start in a saloon or on the street."

"I've learned that the best fight is the quickest fight," Longarm told the bartender. "And I've broken enough knuckles on hard skulls to have learned to use the butt of my pistol to put a fast halt to my opponent."

"You ever whip a man so hard with a pistol his brains started to leak out of his nose, mouth, and ears?"

"Nope, thank God," Longarm said. "But a few times I've come close."

Sam was bored and wanted to talk. "I saw a fella named Bill Washburn get his brains made into hash. Happened right where you're standing. A big old man hit Bill with a full bottle of whiskey right between the eyes. Bottle didn't break, but Bill's head broke, and he ain't never been right since."

Longarm had heard this account more times than he cared to remember. "The man that hit him was named Clyde Underwood and he's doing six years in prison. Last

I heard, Clyde had been nearly gutted to death and he isn't much of a man anymore."

"Well he was something to behold when I saw him, I'll tell you. I would have given a day's wages to have seen you and Clyde tangle in this saloon."

Longarm stifled a yawn and shook his head. "I knew Clyde and wanted no part of him. I'd have brained Clyde or shot him in the knee to end that fight quick."

"I've seen you use that Colt in a cross-draw, and you're about as fast and accurate as they come, Marshal."

"There are always faster men . . . and tougher," Longarm told the bartender. "So far I'm just happy I haven't come across any of them yet."

"Maybe you should try your hand at being a full-time gambler."

But Longarm shook his head. "A gambler's life is even more risky than a lawman's. Besides, as we both know, the cards run hot and cold. It's not the life for me, Sam."

"Well, me neither," the bartender admitted. "There was a time about twenty years ago when I considered being a Mississippi riverboat gambler. I heard that some of them can make a thousand dollars in a single night. They bet big on them paddle-wheel steamers, Custis. I heard that they bet real big."

"I expect that is true."

"And I've heard that there are some of the most beautiful whores you ever saw on them big Mississippi paddle wheelers. Those Southern whores will take you to heaven and then drop you back in hell come time to get off the boat in New Orleans. I heard that they are called Creoles and are the prettiest and best . . ."

Longarm had often heard Sam start to rhapsodize about

the steamboat women, and he didn't care to hear that talk again on such a hot afternoon, so he just waved over his shoulder and pushed outside.

There were heat waves dancing off Colfax Avenue, and he felt a little dizzy in the bright, hot sunlight. Taking a deep breath, Longarm started toward Cherry Creek, noting that the blistered city streets were almost empty. That made sense, and he knew that no one with any good sense would be out and about this afternoon. Instead, they would all be holed up inside or down by the creek where the water cooled the air just a mite.

Twenty minutes later, Longarm found a good spot in the shade of a cottonwood tree and removed his coat, which he then folded and used as a pillow. He loosened his string tie and put his hat over his face. Almost instantly, he began to softly snore.

"Help! Help!"

Longarm was roused out of his late-afternoon nap by shrill cries, and he sat up, hand instinctively going to the gun on his left hip. Momentarily caught between sleep and wakefulness, he peered around searching for a lady in distress.

"No!" the woman cried, her voice thick with terror. "Please don't shoot me, Horace!"

Longarm saw a woman leap out from behind some bushes near the creek with the front of her dress torn to the waist and the hem of her skirt twisted high up around her knees. Close behind her, a heavyset and bearded man came barreling out of the bushes in hot pursuit with his pants unbuttoned and his manhood very much standing at attention.

"Come back here, you bitch!" Horace cursed.

The woman was running for her life.

"Over here!" Longarm shouted, drawing his gun and taking aim on the man.

The woman saw Longarm and angled sharply in his direction. Her face was a mask of fear and her hair was littered with twigs and leaves. Longarm saw that she was at least thirty years of age and extremely attractive. The woman had long, loose red hair, a full and bouncy bosom, and ruby-red lips.

"Damn you, Rose! You come back here!" the burly man shouted.

Rose tripped over the torn hem of her skirt and tumbled across the grass. Horace must not have seen Longarm yet, because his entire focus was on the woman. And despite his bulk, Longarm could see that he was fast and determined. Longarm watched Rose regain her feet, but the man was closing and he had a Bowie knife clenched in his fist.

"Freeze!" Longarm shouted.

Horace's close-set eyes turned to him, and then the man shouted a curse and grabbed Rose's hair while he twisted her head back and prepared to slit the woman's throat from ear to ear.

Longarm's pistol was up and he fired as fast as he could pull the trigger. Five shots in the space of two . . . maybe just three seconds, and every one of them struck Horace's face, neck, or upper torso. The knife in his hand jumped away as if it were repelled by what it had nearly been forced to do to the helpless woman, and then Horace was squirting blood like a sieve as he collapsed on her, nearly drowning her in his bright, glistening gore.

Longarm ran over to the woman and hauled the dead man from atop her body. "Miss, are you all right?"

For a moment she didn't answer, and because her eyes were closed he thought that she had fainted. But then her eyes snapped open and she wiped the dead man's blood from her face and began to weep.

"Here," Longarm said, reaching down and helping her to her feet. "Let's walk over to the creek and get you cleaned off."

"Did you kill him?"

"I had no choice," Longarm told her. "He would have slit your throat."

"I know."

"What . . . what were you doing with him in those willows?"

"I was . . ." Her eyes dropped down and she pursed her lips together.

"Never mind," Longarm said, knowing the answer to his insensitive question. "I'm not judging anyone. But I am a Deputy United States Marshal, and there will be an inquiry here, and I'll have to put what happened in writing. So will you, Miss . . ."

"Miss Delamonte," she said. "My name is Rose Delamonte."

"Well, Rose, I'm just glad that I was here when you burst out of those bushes. That man was crazy with anger. Mind telling me why?"

"He . . . he wanted me to marry him," Rose said. "Yes. He was after my hand in marriage, but I didn't love him, and when I refused his offer, Horace became enraged. He . . . he tried to rape me. Force me to do unspeakable things and I had no choice but to run for my life."

"That was evident enough," Longarm told her. "What was the man's last name?"

"Ramsey. His name was Horace Ramsey, and he was from Santa Fe, New Mexico."

Longarm glanced back over his shoulder at the dead man, who was now surrounded by a noisy and curious crowd of gawkers. "Well," Longarm said, turning back to the woman. "I'd better go back over there and get someone to go for a mortician. In this heat, Horace is going to bloat up pretty quick."

Rose Delamonte nodded. "He will," she said. "The bastard deserves to lie there in the heat and rot!"

Longarm wasn't too surprised by the depth of her anger, for after all, the man had tried to rape her and then to cut her throat. Even so, he said, "Just wait here a few minutes, Miss Delamonte. I'll be right back as soon as I get things over there under control."

"I can't thank you enough," she said, voice quavering.

"Any good man would have done exactly the same that I did to save your life," Longarm replied. "Just sit here beside the creek and wash yourself off as best you can and I'll be right back."

"I will," she promised.

But several minutes later, when Longarm was finished with the crowd and the body, he turned to see that Rose Delamonte was gone.

Chapter 2

Longarm knocked on Miss Lucy Crabtree's door, and when it opened she looked very peeved. "You told me you'd be here by six o'clock and you're two hours late!"

"Sorry," Longarm muttered, removing his hat and entering her big apartment.

Lucy was a florist, and she owned a thriving business right downtown, less than one block from the Colorado State Capitol Building. And because of that, her expensive apartment always smelled sweet with fresh bouquets of whatever flowers were available. She also made at least twice the money that Longarm earned and could be counted on to pay for their restaurant meals and drinks. Lucy could be a little irritating and overbearing at times, but she was exceptionally good in bed and really quite a generous and agreeable person . . . except when he was late.

"You're two hours late tonight and you look rumpled and disheveled." She looked him up and down and didn't look pleased. "Custis, there are even grass stains on the knees of your trousers."

"Yeah, I know. I'm not up to my usual standards, but it's been one hell of a hard Sunday."

"And it could get even worse if you don't give me a plausible explanation for your tardiness."

"Lucy, I had to shoot a man to death this afternoon along Cherry Creek," Longarm said bluntly. "How about pouring us a stiff drink?"

She headed for the cabinet where she kept her good liquor. Looking over her shoulder as she poured Longarm a double shot of Wild Goose Whiskey, the best that money could buy, Lucy said, "I'm sorry that I snapped at you. But why on earth . . ."

"It's a long and not very pretty story," he replied, taking the whiskey and raising his glass. "And I expect that you are famished."

"Actually, I had some delicious smoked salmon and crackers about an hour ago, so I'm not hungry at all. Are you?"

"No," he said, tossing some of the Wild Goose down and savoring the warm glow of it as it washed into his stomach. "I find that killing a man usually kills my appetite."

"Small wonder, you poor man," she said, sitting beside him and resting her hand on his muscular thigh. "Do you want to tell me what happened?"

"The man I shot was trying to rape a woman, and when she resisted he went after her with a Bowie knife. I just happened to be the closest person around and there was no choice but to shoot him."

"What about the woman? Was she a prostitute?"

"I don't know," he admitted. "She was, of course, terrified. It was a very close call."

"Did this woman give you her name or the name of the man that was after her?"

"Yes. She told me that her name was Rose Delamonte. The man that I shot to death was named Horace Ramsey, and she told me that he was from Santa Fe, New Mexico."

"Rose Delamonte." Lucy shook her head, looking very skeptical. "Sounds exactly like the kind of name that some whore would use to try and sound exciting or exotic. Did she look like a whore?"

"She simply looked plain scared to death," Longarm answered. "The poor woman was covered with blood because the man I shot five times fell on her and—"

Lucy's fingers flew to her lips. "Did I hear you correctly when you said that you shot him *five times*?"

"Yeah." Longarm drank deeply then swirled the amber whiskey around in his glass before speaking. "I emptied my Colt on him because he was moving so fast and I didn't want to take the chance that I'd miss. Lucy, the man was right on top of her. He grabbed her hair, pulled it back, and was an instant away from slitting the poor woman's throat!"

"Sounds like I had better pour you a refill right away," Lucy said, coming to her feet and bringing a crystal decanter which she placed in front of him on an ivory-inlaid table. "So after you shot the man dead, what happened?"

"I took the woman over to the creek and attempted to wash off all the blood."

"Was she naked?" Lucy asked, eyeing him closely.

"No. But her dress was badly torn and it looked like she had a nasty bruise on her cheek."

"So what happened next?"

"I told Rose Delamonte to wait for me while I dispersed

a gathering crowd of gawkers and sent someone for a mortician. But when I was finished with that, the woman was gone."

Lucy raised an eyebrow. "You saved this woman's life and in repayment she just . . . disappeared?"

"That's right. But in her defense, she was badly shaken up and looked pretty awful with all the blood and her torn dress. I'm sure she just wanted to run away from all the people staring at her."

"I'll bet anything she was just a downtown prostitute trying to make a few bucks in the weeds," Lucy pronounced.

"I don't know," Longarm said, shaking his head. "I'd never seen her before."

"Well, I shouldn't think so," Lucy said, sounding a little shocked. "After all, why would you be looking at whores when I'm giving you all that you need that way?"

"You're right."

Lucy pressed her body closer. "Finish that whiskey and let's skip going out to dinner tonight. I want to make you forget that awful experience, and later I can rustle around and make us a good meal."

Longarm wasn't really up for lovemaking, but when Lucy began to rub his crotch and nibble on his earlobe, he changed his mind.

He finished his whiskey as Lucy was preparing herself in the bedroom. She lived on the third floor of a very upscale hotel building. Her apartment had a magnificent view of Denver, and now the gaslights were illuminating the downtown and the city was starting to look almost magical. The brutal afternoon heat had abated, and when Longarm looked down at the street he could see that people were out and about.

"Custis?"

He turned and smiled to see Lucy dressed in a white silk negligee and holding a red rose to her lips.

"Custis, why don't you come join me right now."

Longarm swallowed hard. Lucy Crabtree was a gorgeous brunette, and she had a body that would make any man salivate. "Sounds like the best idea I've heard all day," he told her. "Did you go to the shop today?"

"Yes, I did. There was an afternoon wedding at the Episcopal Church and we supplied all the floral arrangements. It was a very expensive wedding, and I simply had to be there to make sure that everything went well . . . and that I was paid as promised. The father of the bride was so pleased that he gave me a very generous tip."

"I'll bet he did. You probably made more money in one day than I make in two weeks."

"Probably," Lucy said with a shrug of her shoulders to signify that these things did not matter to her. "But let's not talk about work or money. In fact, my big, handsome marshal, let's not talk at all."

Longarm drank the rest of his Wild Goose Whiskey and placed his glass on the table. He began to undress as he walked toward Lucy, who was backing up toward her bedroom.

"My oh my," she said as he lay down beside her and began to stroke her most sensitive and private parts, "you sure are a handsome stud."

"And you, Lucy, are a sprightly and pretty filly."

"So mount me and make me shout at the ceiling," she whispered, voice thick with desire. "I've been looking forward to this all day long."

Longarm mounted Lucy and began to move his hips just the way that she liked. In no time at all, Lucy was moaning with pleasure and Longarm was grinning wolfishly as his passion quickly rose.

Soon, they were both howling with pleasure and gasping for air. Longarm slammed his seed home and Lucy shuddered and stifled a cry of joy into her pillow, while her hips kept pumping for the last bit of ecstasy that could be milked from their sweaty, frenetic sexual union.

Chapter 3

"So," Marshal Billy Vail said, running his stubby fingers through his thinning hair and eyeing his favorite deputy with a frown. "If I understand you correctly, you were taking a nap along Cherry Creek yesterday when this beautiful woman burst out of the bushes while being pursued by a man with a Bowie knife?"

"Yep," Longarm replied.

"And she was yelling, 'Help! Help!' so you jumped up and shot the man who was after her, and his name was Horace Ramsey and he was supposedly from Santa Fe, New Mexico."

"That's what the red-haired victim named Rose Delamonte told me."

"But she disappeared . . . like vapor."

"I'm afraid that is also correct. It took me a few minutes to disperse the crowd and find someone willing to go find a mortician. And when I was through with that, I turned around and she was gone."

"And you'd never seen her before?"

"Never." Longarm paused for a moment, then added, "Billy, this woman was absolutely stunning."

"I bet she was a prostitute."

"I don't think so."

"Well," Billy said, steepling his fingers, "she couldn't have been a *lad*y or she would never have gotten into the weeds with a murderous brute."

"Maybe you're right."

"Any idea where we can find this Rose Delamonte?"

"Nope."

Billy's brow furrowed. "Tell you what. Let's go out in the office and I'll call for everyone to listen up while you describe this woman, and maybe someone has seen or even screwed her."

"Okay," Longarm said. "But I just have the feeling that she is new to town and she is not a prostitute."

"Custis, I've never understood it, but in the matter of beautiful women you have a trusting and surprisingly innocent heart," Billy remarked.

"I was raised to appreciate the opposite sex . . . and to respect them unless they proved they deserved no respect," Longarm told his boss. "Billy, I regard all women as ladies, and long ago I discovered that when you treat them that way, that's how they almost always behave."

"Interesting but rather a childish theory," Billy drawled as he pushed out of his office chair and headed for his door.

Ten minutes later they were back in Billy's office. "No one seems to have seen the woman whose description you provided."

"I didn't expect that they would have," Longarm replied. "Like I told you, I think Rose Delamonte is new to this town."

"Find her," Billy ordered. "In order to resolve this shooting and get it all recorded and laid to rest, we need to find the woman and we need to learn more about the man that you shot . . . *five fucking times.*"

"Billy," Longarm said, holding up his hand. "I know that sounds like overkill but . . ."

"Damn right it does!"

"Listen," Longarm said, "I had but an instant to act and shoot. The target was in motion and his knife was raised to slash Miss Delamonte's lovely throat. I couldn't take the chance that one or two bullets might not prove instantly fatal, and that is why I emptied my revolver. If you'd have been there as I was, I'm sure you would have done exactly the same thing."

"Perhaps," Billy conceded. "But I also would have made sure the woman was in sight so that she didn't disappear."

"There were probably other witnesses."

"By any chance did you think to write down their names and addresses so that they could be called if necessary?"

"No," Longarm admitted. "I did not. I thought that Miss Delamonte would provide all the information that was needed."

"Well, Custis, this time you thought wrong. And I know the city authorities aren't going to simply let us off the hook without some answers and witnesses. You are well aware that they do not like us feds and are jealous of the pay and working conditions that we enjoy."

"Yeah, I know that."

"Then find the woman and hopefully a few of the witnesses so that we can put this killing to bed and not have to worry about any repercussions."

"What repercussions are we talking about?"

Billy shrugged. "The dead man must have friends and family. If there is any doubt about this killing, then they can make things sticky for my department and for you."

"I understand."

"Find her, Custis. Find her before she leaves Denver just as mysteriously as she arrived in our city."

"You could also send a telegram to Santa Fe asking the authorities there if they know a man named Horace Ramsey or any members of his family."

"I'll compose a quick message and you can go to Western Union and send it off immediately. With luck, we'll hear back from the marshal's office in Santa Fe this afternoon."

Longarm came out of his chair and forced a smile. "You're always about one step ahead of me, Billy. That's why you make the big money around here and I stay a lowly deputy marshal."

"Bullshit!" Billy scoffed. "And don't you dare try to appease me with false flattery."

Longarm picked up his snuff-brown Stetson, placed it just right on his head, and yawned as he prepared to go.

"You look tired this morning," Billy observed. "I suppose you didn't sleep all that well after what happened down by the creek."

"Yeah," Longarm said, choosing not to tell him how he and Lucy Crabtree had made love three times in the night and once again after waking this morning.

"After you find Miss Delamonte," Billy said, following him out to the office and laying a paternal hand on his shoulder, "I think we ought to give you a week of well-deserved vacation time."

"I'd like that a lot," Custis told him. "This heat is really getting me down and I'll go up in the mountains, where I know a man with a cabin and a pretty daughter that I've wanted to get to know a whole lot better."

"Gawdammit, Custis!" Billy complained with unconcealed disapproval. "Screwing women of all shapes, ages, and sizes is about all you can ever think of!"

"Better than thinking about how I nearly blew a man's head off his shoulders yesterday," Longarm snapped on his way out the door.

Chapter 4

Rose Delamonte sat on her hotel room bed with her head cradled in her hands as she tried to calm herself. What was she going to do now? Horace had almost killed her . . . and would have slit her throat if that big man hadn't shot him dead. Even while Horace lay in a pool of fresh blood, the big man had told her that he was a United States marshal. And all he had asked of her was to wait until he dispersed the crowd and sent for an undertaker.

But she *hadn't* waited. No, that would have been a terrible mistake, and she had made enough mistakes for one day.

Rose went over yesterday's terrible killing again and again in her mind. She had come from Santa Fe to entrap Horace. To somehow make him sign a confession to the murder of her young husband and his parents, and the forging of papers giving the Ramsey family their ranchland. How naïve she was to think that Horace, who had always wanted her for his own wife, could be persuaded,

by whatever means, to tell the truth and go against his rich
and powerful family.

She had lured him to the cool banks of Cherry Creek,
not sure what she was going to do but prepared to do anything in her power . . . *anything* . . . to make him tell the
truth about what his family had done to her poor husband.
But he had been drinking, and so nothing she tried to say
or do persuaded him. The carefully written confession she
had wanted him to sign was still folded in her pocket.
When she had presented it to him and pleaded for his help
and sense of justice . . . he had become enraged.

And vicious.

In the thick creek-side willows he had thrown her down
and tried to brutally rape her. When she fought him, he
began to use his fists and then he brought out his Bowie
knife. After that, everything was pretty much a blur. Somehow, Rose had managed to bite his lip so hard that she had
nearly torn it from his face, and then she had rolled over
into the mud and scrambled away. Horace, bloody and in a
rage, had come after her, and when she saw a man napping
under a tree she cried out in desperation.

And that man had been her savior. A big, deadly lawman.
A man who acted in a split second and saved her life by
killing Horace Ramsey in little more than the blink of an eye.

Now that lawman would be looking for her, seeking
answers. Rose knew that she should turn herself in and try
to explain what she had done. She could show the authorities the confession she had written for Horace Ramsey to
sign. A confession that if she had gotten it signed would
have put the Ramsey family in prison to the last man and
given her back the land that her father-in-law had given to
her and her new husband. But now . . . now what?

Rose knew one thing with dead certainty, and that was

that once the news of Horace's death reached Santa Fe, Ramsey men would be coming to Denver bent on killing both her and the big marshal.

So how could she run and leave the unsuspecting lawman to an almost certain death?

The answer, Rose Delamonte knew, was that she could not. She would have to alert the marshal and go on the run herself to some place she had never been before. An unfamiliar place where they would never find and kill her.

There was a knock on Rose's door and it startled her badly. Could the Denver authorities have already tracked her down? She sat very still and hoped that whoever was at the door would give up and go away.

But the knocking grew louder. Finally, Rose decided that someone must *know* she was in her room. Taking a derringer from a bedside drawer, she checked it to make sure that it was ready before she called, "Who is it?"

"Marshal Custis Long. Miss Delamonte, I know you're in there because the desk clerk told me so. Now, will you please open the door?"

She recognized his voice and knew that it would be futile not to answer.

"Just a minute," she said, pulling on a dress that she had taken off because of the stifling heat in her room.

Rose kept the gun held tightly in her fist as she unlocked her door, and when she opened it there her savior stood filling the doorway with his broad shoulders.

"You didn't wait yesterday like I told you," Longarm said, brows knit together in disapproval.

"How did you find me so quickly?"

He shrugged. "With that red hair and your beauty, I knew it wouldn't be hard. Men remember you . . . and so do women."

"I see."

His eyes fell to the pistol in her fist. "Are you going to try and shoot me, or yourself?"

The way he said it, with just the hint of a smile, made her relax. "Neither," she told him.

"Can I come inside and talk with you?"

"If I said no, you'd come in anyway, wouldn't you?"

"I guess I'd have to," Longarm replied. "I killed a man yesterday to save your life. I'd think that the least I deserve is some thanks and an explanation."

"Thanks. And come inside."

Longarm entered the room. It was small but nice, just as he'd expect in one of Denver's better hotels. He glanced around, looking for any personal items that Rose would have that might tell him something about her, but he saw nothing of interest.

She motioned toward the only chair in the room and he sat, removing his hat. "Nice room."

"Yes. I'd offer you some kind of refreshment, but I have none. You look like you're suffering from the heat."

His shirt was damp and he mopped his brow with his sleeve. "I can't remember when it's been this hot in Denver. I don't do well in the heat. Once I was offered a town marshal's job down by Tombstone, but I knew the heat would get to me."

When she didn't say anything, Longarm added, "But I realize that Santa Fe is higher and probably cooler."

"About like Denver."

Longarm cleared his throat. "All right," he said, "enough of the small talk. Why don't you just tell me everything that happened and why Horace Ramsey was trying to kill you."

"If I told you the truth, I doubt that you'd believe me."

"And why, Miss Delamonte, would you say that?"

"Because I have no proof to explain the reason I came to Denver and the reason I was with Horace Ramsey yesterday."

Longarm studied his hat, ran a forefinger and thumb along the edge of its flat brown brim. "Miss Delamonte, can I . . ."

"*Mrs.* Delamonte," she corrected. "I was married to Jesse Delamonte in Santa Fe almost one year ago, but he was killed."

"Sorry."

"Now . . . now I am a widow. My husband inherited a ranch from his father and mother, who were killed under very suspicious circumstances."

"How so?"

"They were in a buggy and it ran off the side of a mountain."

"That can happen, ma'am."

"Jesse's father was an expert horseman and a very fine driver." Rose lifted her chin. "He was not a man to risk his wife's life doing something foolish. Someone had to have forced him and his wife over the side of the cliff."

"Did the Santa Fe authorities investigate?"

"Of course. But there was no proof that any wrongdoing had occurred. The day that Mr. and Mrs. Delamonte died, it had been raining, so the road they were traveling was slick."

"Then maybe it really was an accident," Longarm suggested.

"It was not! I knew my father-in-law, and he would never have put himself or his wife in danger."

"But you just told me that the road they were traveling was slick."

"And wide. Wide enough for two more wagons to pass

with room to spare. And the pair of horses that were pull-ing the carriage were very well trained and not in the least likely to spook and go off a cliff."

Longarm glanced around the room, trying to think of a way to get this conversation back on track. His eyes landed on a pitcher and glass by the bedside.

"Any water in that pitcher, Mrs. Delamonte? My poor throat is as dry as sand."

"There's only that one glass, but I don't think you'll contract anything from my use of it."

"Thanks."

Longarm poured himself a glass and chugged it down. He rotated the pitcher and felt that it was still quite full, so he poured a second glass and drank that one right down, too.

"You *were* thirsty," she said. "Sorry I don't have any-thing stronger than water."

"I can wait until this evening for a few drinks. But let's get back to the subject of the shooting. I have to know who this Horace Ramsey was and why he was trying to cut your throat."

"He lusted for me very badly, and Horace was a man who took what he wanted. I fought him off, managed to run, and that's where you came into the picture and saved my life."

Longarm cleared his throat and replaced his glass on the table. It was time to ask the blunt, hard question. "Mrs. Delamonte, were you with this Horace Ramsey fella to make money?"

She actually was able to smile. "What a delicate and tactful way to ask me if I am a whore."

Longarm shifted in his chair uncomfortably. "Ma'am, I just have to know what was going on. I killed a man.

There are reports to write and there might even be relatives from Santa Fe that will be demanding answers."

Rose shook her head sadly. "Oh, they'll want a lot more than answers from you."

"And exactly what does that mean?"

"You killed the eldest son of a very important Santa Fe family, and they will have their blood revenge."

Longarm sighed. "Not if I tell them that their eldest son was trying to slit your throat."

"Wrong!" Rose lowered her voice. "Marshal, you have no idea what the Ramsey family is capable of doing for money or revenge."

"So then tell me how it is and tell me straight."

Rose thought a moment and then reached for the confession that she had naïvely thought Horace might sign in exchange for her sexual favors for as long as he wanted them. "Please read this, Marshal."

The confession was blunt and straight to the point. It said that the Ramsey family had forced the carriage off the cliff in order to gain control of the Delamonte family ranch and that furthermore they had killed Rose's husband, Jesse Delamonte.

Longarm read the unsigned confession twice. "And you actually thought that Horace would sign this?"

"I thought that I could get him drunk on whiskey and passion and make him do what I wanted. I was almost successful, but at the last moment, when I spread the confession out on my . . . my bare thigh . . . Horace balked. He went crazy, and that's when I knew my life was about to end if I didn't get away from the man."

"Mrs. Delamonte, you must have a very high opinion of your persuasive powers."

"Please call me Rose."

"All right. And I'm Custis."

"As for your statement about my opinion of myself, I do recognize I am attractive," she admitted without turning her eyes away in embarrassment. "In fact, it was said by most that I was the prettiest young woman in Santa Fe when I chose Jesse to become my husband. And while I know it sounds awful, I did break more than a few hearts when the announcement was made in the newspaper. And the heart that was broken into the most pieces belonged to . . ."

"Horace Ramsey," Longarm said, finishing her sentence.

"Exactly."

"And now that my boss has sent a telegram to Santa Fe asking for information on either you or Mr. Ramsey . . ."

Her hand flew to her mouth. "He did that *already*?"

"Well of course he did," Longarm said. "If you'd have stayed with me and told me what you just said, then we might have waited and talked things out a bit . . . but with you suddenly missing there wasn't any choice. We needed answers. Answers that could not wait. The body has to be attended to. Someone has to decide what shall be done with it and—"

"Throw it down your city sewer," Rose said bitterly. "Horace and his family were in on the murder of my husband and his parents, who were good, honest, and hard-working people!"

"I'm sure that they were."

For a few moments, both Longarm and the woman sat in stony silence, until finally Rose said, "I'll make a formal statement. Sign anything you want me to sign. But make no mistake about it, Marshal. The moment that a telegram arrives in Santa Fe asking those questions about me and Horace Ramsey, evil will be set in motion. Men will come to kill us both."

"This isn't Santa Fe, Rose. I'm a federal officer of the law and I am not afraid of anyone."

"Then you are as good as dead already," she said flatly. "And I say that not in any derogatory context. I saw you pull your gun and I witnessed how good you are at killing. But the Ramsey men are murderers. They won't come straight up at you in broad daylight. They will ambush you, and if that fails, they will find out where you live and perhaps jump you and throw you off a building. Or hire someone to poison you."

Longarm scowled. "You sound pretty sure of what you're saying."

"I am *very* sure of what I'm saying. If you stay and wait here in Denver, you will die."

"And you as well."

"Yes," she told him. "There is only·one choice to be made for me and that is to run."

"Run to where?"

"I have no idea. I was considering that very question when you knocked on my door."

"Running is rarely the answer to a problem, Rose."

"I just want to live."

"But how," Longarm asked, "is that going to bring justice to the Delamonte folks whom you swear were murdered?"

"It won't bring them justice," she whispered, voice bitter. "But Jesse would tell me to save myself. And besides, because of me Horace is *dead*. And that, at least, is some small consolation."

Longarm stood up and put his hat back on his head.

The room was on the third floor and very hot. He needed some fresh air. Some cool fresh air and a little time to sort out all that this woman had revealed. Could he trust her to be telling him the truth?

"I need to take you to the Federal Building," he said. "I want you to tell my boss, Marshal Billy Vail, everything you've told me. And I'm sure what you say will be taken down in writing and you will be asked to put your signature on the statement."

"I will do that." She shook her head, and a tear slid down her bruised cheek. "But it won't change a thing, Marshal. If a telegram was sent to Santa Fe, the wheels have been set in motion."

"We can intercept the Ramsey men at the train station."

"They won't come on a damned train."

"Then a stagecoach."

"You still don't understand. They will come like thieves in the night. In ones, twos, and threes. They will come and they will kill us both!"

Longarm's first reaction was to tell her that these killers were coming into *his* town, his jurisdiction, and that they would be . . . if what she said was true, they would be either killed or arrested. He was, after all, not the only federal law officer in Denver. There were at this time no less than seven of them in the federal building. Men like himself who had killed and were prepared to fight and kill again.

But when Longarm studied her bruised yet still lovely face and saw the naked fear in her eyes, he kept his mouth shut.

They would see about these Ramsey men, these thieves in the night and cowardly murderers.

Yes, he thought, they just would wait and see.

Chapter 5

"Please sit down, Mrs. Delamonte," Marshal Billy Vail said. "Can I have someone bring you coffee or water?"

"No, thank you."

"Custis, you can drag a chair in here from the office."

"I'm fine standing," he replied.

"All right then, we might as well get right down to the subject at hand," Billy said. "I understand that you were almost murdered down by Cherry Creek on Sunday afternoon and that my deputy marshal, Custis Long, had to kill your attacker in order to save your life."

"That's right," Rose answered. "And I explained to Marshal Long the reason that Horace Ramsey was trying to kill me."

"Yes, he told me all about that a few minutes ago when we spoke in private," Billy said. "I understand that you even had a confession you were hoping the dead man would sign."

"I have it with me," Rose said, taking the written confession out of her purse and handing it to Billy Vail.

"Unfortunately, Horace refused to sign it and became enraged at my pleas to do so."

Billy read the confession statement and then handed it back to Rose. "I have to ask . . . Did you really expect that man to put his and his entire family's neck in a noose?"

Rose blushed, and it enhanced the fire in her beautiful hair. "I know it sounds stupid, and I suppose it was. But you have to understand that Horace Ramsey wasn't too bright and he did hunger for me in the worst way. When my late husband announced our betrothal, Horace practically went insane. He and Jesse fought and my husband whipped Horace quite severely. After that, and although I didn't realize it at the time, Jesse had signed his own death warrant."

"And there is the matter of the ranch that you say was unlawfully taken from you."

"That's right. After my late husband's death—"

"Excuse me," Longarm interrupted. "How did your husband come to his sad end?"

"He was ambushed one evening while out fixing fence. There were no witnesses, but my father- and mother-in-law knew just as surely as I knew that it was the Ramsey men who had ambushed Jesse."

Silent tears filled Rose's blue eyes and Billy offered her a clean handkerchief. "I know this must be extremely hard on you, Mrs. Delamonte. But we really have to know all the facts."

"There isn't a lot else to say," Rose told both lawmen. "Jesse was bushwhacked and we buried him on the ranch beside the graves of his grandparents. Less than a month later, on a rainy day, my in-laws were going for supplies and their buggy went over the side of a high cliff. I tried to get help from the Santa Fe authorities . . . and while they were sympathetic . . . they know that the Ramsey family owns a lot of land and has powerful political connections all over New Mexico."

"So you don't believe that the authorities in Santa Fe were very interested in stirring things up?"

"That's the way of it," Rose said.

"And how, exactly, did the ranch come into the possession of the Ramsey family?" Billy asked.

"They own the bank that held the mortgage on the ranch. It wasn't a large mortgage, considering what the ranch was worth."

"How much?" Longarm asked.

"Six thousand dollars," Rose answered. "But the ranch was easily worth twenty and that does not include the livestock, all of which disappeared in a few weeks."

"So you," Billy said, "believe the livestock were rustled by the Ramsey family?"

"Of course they were!"

"How many animals are we talking about?" Longarm asked.

"There were about three hundred head of cattle and maybe twenty horses. Both my father-in-law and husband were actually much more interested in horses than the cattle. But Jesse always said that the ranch had made money on the cattle and lost it back on the horses we were breeding."

Longarm frowned. "Wasn't all the stock branded?"

"Of course. But it just so happens that our brand could easily be changed to the Ramsey brand with a running iron."

"How unfortunate," Longarm muttered. "There are some brands that are almost impossible to tell have been altered by rustlers."

"We were going to apply to the state authorities for a new brand to take care of that very problem," Rose told him, biting her lower lip to keep herself under control. "We just never quite got around to it."

Longarm scowled and looked to his boss, who was studying a silver paperweight that he was especially fond of and which had been given to him by the office last Christmas.

"Billy?"

"I'm thinking." Billy sighed then looked up at Rose. "Mrs. Delamonte, I hardly know what to say to you about the ranch and the livestock back in New Mexico. And as for your claim that your husband and his parents were murdered by the Ramsey family . . . well, what proof have you to offer us that this is true?"

"I've not a shred of proof," she said, chin lifting. "I clearly understand that I am a widow without friends or family. I did manage to come away with a good deal of money. The Delamonte family knew that their enemies owned the bank and had ways of cheating them out of money, so they kept gold, coins, jewelry, and cash hidden away on the ranch."

"And you, thank heavens, were able to take that before you left the ranch?" Longarm asked.

"Part of it." Rose cleared her throat and used Billy's handkerchief to loudly blow her nose. "I couldn't take the gold. It was too heavy and I had to leave in a great hurry or I'd have been murdered."

"How much gold did you leave?"

"About five or six pounds of nuggets," she told them.

Longarm whistled. "That's a lot of gold!"

"Yes. It's worth thousands. I was hoping to someday return to the ranch and dig the gold up. But, of course, that would have to be years from now and only after I was sure that the ranch was unoccupied or that I could find someone trustworthy enough to dig up the gold for a generous share of the value."

"But you don't know such a man," Longarm said.

"No, I don't. Anyone living in or around Santa Fe would instantly understand that they were putting their lives in great jeopardy by going onto the ranch with a shovel and hoping to go unnoticed."

"Is it buried right near the ranch house?" Billy blurted.

"Not far," she said vaguely. "Not far at all. And it's in a place where it will never be accidentally unearthed."

"Whew! Billy whistled. "This is one of the most interesting stories and situations I've come across in many a day, and I've had my share of interesting cases."

Rose wiped her cheeks dry and said, "I told Custis that his life would be very much in danger when the family discovered it was he who shot Horace to death. My life, of course, is already in danger. The Ramsey family is large and well scattered in New Mexico. They seem to be everywhere and have connections in the highest places."

Billy wagged a finger. "This isn't New Mexico, and I assure you that those people have no power in Colorado."

"That's why they are even more dangerous," Rose countered. "That's why they will try to kill your brave marshal in a very devious way. Poison, I should think."

Hearing this and remembering the few poisonings he had witnessed, Longarm shuddered. A blade to the belly would be preferable to a slow, agonizing death by poisoning.

Billy was silent for a few moments then said, "I am sure that Custis has told you that I sent off a telegram to the sheriff in Santa Fe asking for information."

"Yes," Rose said, "and I was sad to hear that."

Billy frowned. "Perhaps I should not have sent off the telegram so quickly, but you were missing and we needed some answers from New Mexico."

"I understand that," Rose replied. "But now the Ramsey men know what happened to Horace and where I am. They also know or will know soon the circumstances of Horace's death. All of that will cause them to gather in a quick council and then to come here to exact their revenge."

"And we will, of course, either arrest or kill them when they arrive," Billy said.

"If only I could believe that to be true," Rose told both lawmen. "But I don't."

"Perhaps you seriously underestimate us," Billy said a little defensively.

"And perhaps you seriously underestimate the cunning and determination of the Ramsey men, as well as their women," Rose countered.

"So what should we do?" Longarm asked, wearying of the back-and-forth discussion.

"I'm thinking," Billy replied. "You are both . . . if what Mrs. Delamonte says is absolutely true . . . the targets."

"Bait," Longarm added.

"Yes, bait," Billy agreed. "And as bait, you will be drawing these people to you on *our ground*."

"So we just sit tight?"

Billy shrugged. "What is the alternative? If you run and hide, then we gain nothing, and I know that running and hiding isn't even a part of your vocabulary, Custis."

Longarm turned to Rose. "How long will these people be in their 'council' as you call it?"

"Less than one day."

"Then they'll come directly to Denver and that would take them less than five days."

"They won't come all together," Rose told both men. "They will come singly, in pairs, and maybe in threes. And . . ." she added, "they might even bring a few of their women as insurance."

"Their women would come to kill you and Custis?" Billy asked in obvious disbelief.

"Yes, they would."

"Jesus," Billy whispered. "I hope that what you're telling us isn't as bad as you make it out to be."

"It will be that bad," Rose promised.

"We'll need descriptions of every man among them and perhaps even a few of the women that you think might be coming," Billy said. "I will circulate those descriptions in this office and have them forwarded to the local sheriff's office as well. We will be on the lookout for them to arrive in three to five days."

"I'm a fair artist," Rose said. "I'll not only give you descriptions of the brothers and a few of the worst relatives, but I'll try and draw them."

"Excellent!" Billy said. "Now, where are you staying?"

She told him.

"Nice hotel, but I think you had better relocate to a safer haven."

"What," Longarm asked, "do you have in mind?"

"I don't have anything in mind yet," Billy admitted. "I'll put some serious thought to it, though."

"The room next to mine has just been vacated," Longarm offered. "There was an old coot named Charlie that lived there, but he died a few days ago, and now there is just his cat, also named Charlie, which I have to feed until I can find it a home."

"Oh," Billy said, shaking his head, "I'm not sure that it would be wise to put you both in such close proximity."

"I like cats," Rose said. "And I would feel safer being near Custis."

Billy shook his head and Longarm knew exactly what his boss was thinking. Same thing as he was thinking, but neither of them would voice their thoughts.

Rose looked from one to the other and then said, "What is wrong with that arrangement?"

"Nothing," Longarm said innocently.

She looked at Billy until he shrugged his narrow shoulders and said, "If you're comfortable with that arrangement, then why not?"

"Yes," Longarm said, vaguely wondering how Lucy Crabtree would take this news when she discovered that a beautiful young woman in danger of her life was living right next to him.

Oh well, he thought, Lucy had been getting much too serious about their relationship lately anyway.

Chapter 6

Longarm knocked on the door of the rooming house manager, an old hag named Aggie who strongly disapproved of him and considered him a sex-crazed degenerate.

"Yeah, what do you want?" she demanded, smoking a thin cigar in her old bathrobe and slippers.

Longarm forced a smile. "I found you a new tenant for Charlie's room, Aggie."

"Is that so?" the old woman replied, staring at him suspiciously. "And who would that be?"

"A lady that needs a place to stay for a while."

"That's just what I thought," Aggie croaked, inhaling deeply off the stinking cigar. "You want a woman close, but not so close that you don't have room for other women to come spend time bouncin' on their buttocks."

Longarm really couldn't stand this old battle-axe, but the rent was cheap and his room suited him very well so he managed to say, "This woman is from out of town. She won't be staying more than a few weeks."

"Well, I don't need the rent money that bad and besides,"

Aggie added, "I think I already got the room rented to a man who sells food out of a little cart on Colfax Avenue. His name i . . ."

"George," Longarm said. "And you don't want George in this building because he'll steal the shirt off your back . . . or in your case the bathrobe . . . if you aren't watching him."

"Is that a fact?"

"That is definitely a fact, Aggie. Now, I've brought this lady and she's waiting right outside if you'd like to meet her."

"She a low-class whore?"

"Hell no!"

"Then how'd she get to know the likes of you?" Addie demanded.

"Dammit, I don't consort with whores."

"And my mother died a virgin."

Aggie blew a cloud of stinking smoke in his face which Longarm waved off. "Here," he said, reaching into his pocket for his own cigars. "Take one of these and give your lungs and the air a break."

Aggie snatched the cigar from his hand, ran it by her nose, and nodded with approval. "Not bad. Okay, has this woman got any money to pay me for moving in for a while or do you have to poke her a few times for rent money?"

"I'm sure that she does have her own money."

"Let me see some cash and the woman and then I'll decide."

"You sure are hard to help out with a new renter," Longarm complained. "I'll go get her right now."

He went outside, to where Rose Delamonte was waiting. "I told my landlady about you and she wants to meet you. You'd also better have some cash to give her."

"I have cash. How much?"

"I don't know. She charges me ten dollars a month."

"That seems reasonable."

"I doubt you'll be here long," he told her.

Rose nodded in agreement. "I might if I'm not dead by then."

"She's a real bitch and she thinks all I know are loose women," Longarm warned.

"Sounds like a jewel," Rose told him. "Let's get this over with so I can meet that cat named Charlie and get cleaned up and moved in."

"The room is furnished, but . . ."

"I'll buy some things of my own. A new bed for starters. Was this old guy named Charlie clean?"

"He wasn't too bad," Longarm said. "I liked the guy and hated to see him ship out so unexpectedly."

Rose went into the building with Longarm following in her wake. She walked right up to Aggie and said, "I am Mrs. Rose Delamonte and I need a place to stay for a few weeks."

"Why not a hotel?" Aggie demanded, looking her up and down. "You're dressed nice. Looks like you could afford a nice hotel."

Rose took her time in replying, and Longarm knew that she was way too smart to tell Aggie that her life was in danger and they were waiting for New Mexico men to come and try to kill both her and Longarm. So instead of the whole truth, Rose said, "I need a place where I can't easily be found."

Aggie snorted and gave her a superior look. "Runnin'

from Mr. Delamonte, I suppose, while you're doin' it with the handsome federal marshal?"

"No," Rose snapped. "I'm recently widowed."

Aggie blinked with surprise, and her craggy, wrinkled old face softened just ever so much. "Your husband just died?"

"That's right. And we were very much in love."

Aggie swallowed. "Well I lost my husband sixteen years ago. Bert was lazy as a boar hog and about as smelly, too. But I miss the old bastard to this day so I'm sorry for your loss."

"Thank you."

Aggie said. "I'm sure that Custis here has told you that I charge ten dollars a month for a room. That's for longtime renters. For short-time renters it is fifty cents a day and you can use the bath at the end of the hall once a week. I have a boy that brings hot water from the basement. You just have to let him know. If you want a bath more than once a week, you'll have to pay the boy a dollar for haulin' the hot water up the stairs and firin' up the boiler."

"I want a bath this evening," Rose said. "And I'll pay for two weeks' rent in advance plus the extra bath plus a little extra for your kindness and silence about who I am and why I'm here."

Rose handed the landlady ten dollars. Aggie stared at it and then said, "This is a whole month's rent."

"Keep the money just in case."

"In case of what?" Aggie asked, not a bit uppity or acting superior anymore.

"In case something bad happens to me," Rose said. "Now, can I have a key to the room?"

"Be right back," Aggie said, turning and moving faster than Longarm had ever seen her move before.

"Here you go," Aggie said, handing her a key. "And don't you worry. Besides the marshal here, we've got plenty of watchful eyes in this building. If any strangers come askin' for you, I'll tell them you ain't here and ain't never been here, either."

"Thank you," Rose said, giving the old woman a warm smile.

"You are welcome, young lady. And if you get lonesome or need something, you just come down and knock on my door. Even if it is to unburden yourself of your recent sorrow."

"You are very kind. Mrs. . . ."

"Aggie." She shot a glance at Longarm, who was standing behind Rose. "And don't you let that big womanizing galoot into your room if you value your honor."

Rose just smiled and left.

"You leave her alone!" Aggie said, shaking a forefinger at Longarm. "She ain't like most trashy women you bring here."

"I'll be as modest and meek as a choirboy, Aggie," Longarm vowed, crossing his heart and trying not to burst out laughing.

"Get out of here!" Aggie ordered before she slammed her door. "And behave yourself around that girl," she called from behind it.

"Yes, ma'am!"

When they had gotten Rose moved in, she sat down in an overstuffed chair and asked, "Where is that poor, orphaned cat?"

Longarm pointed to the window. "Charlie has been watching you while we got settled."

Rose jumped up and went to open the window. Charlie meowed and fussed and Rose picked him up and carried

him over to the chair, where she began to stroke his fur
and tell him how extraordinarily handsome he was. Longarm just watched in amusement with his arms folded on
his chest. Charlie the cat was about as ordinary a yellow
tabby as you would ever see. One of his ears had been
bitten half off and his tail was short and ratty-looking. But
right now, Charlie was in heaven.

"Thank you for everything, Custis," Rose said. "Please
lock the door on your way out."

"Would you like me to take you out to dinner tonight?"

"No. I'll find a grocery or ask Aggie for something for
myself and for Charlie here, who seems a bit on the skinny
side. We'll just enjoy a quiet evening together."

"You and Charlie?"

"Yes." Rose smiled patiently at him. "I'm a *recently*
widowed woman, Custis. And I'm not a whore or a har-
lot."

"But you were going to do whatever it took to get
Horace Ramsey to sign that confession," he reminded her.

"Yes," she admitted, hurt filling her voice. "But I gave
that long and careful consideration. And if he had signed
my confession, I did put some serious thought into killing
him, if he did not kill me first."

"I understand," Longarm replied, not sure that he did.
"If you need anything, please knock on the wall and I'll
be here in seconds."

"I'll be fine for the next few days, until the Ramsey
men have had enough time to get to Denver. After that,
well, we'll just have to wait and see what happens."

"It's going to be all right," he told her.

"Can you promise me that?"

He took a deep breath. "I can promise that I'll lay down
my life to save yours."

Rose looked up from petting the purring Charlie. "I know you would," she replied. "And I'm grateful."

"Are you sure I can't bring you something to eat? I could get something cooked and bring it up here for us and . . ."

"Thank you, but no. Do you know where I can buy a new bed?"

"You'll only be here a short while and . . ."

"Please, I have plenty of money to buy a new bed and sheets and a few other things to make this room feel more like it belongs to me than to the late gentleman who owned sweet Charlie."

"I understand," Longarm said, then told her where to buy a bed, groceries, and whatever else she needed.

"I'll see you tomorrow," she told him.

"Breakfast?"

"All right. But not too early."

"Eight o'clock okay?"

"Nine is better."

Longarm knew that would mean that he would arrive at the office at least two hours late, but he didn't care. Billy Vail understood the seriousness of Rose's predicament and he would give Longarm all the time he needed to be with and protect her.

Maybe, he thought, I can talk her into having dinner tomorrow night and then . . .

Chapter 7

The sheriff of Santa Fe was a congenial and handsome man in his late fifties named Lucas Mandrake Greer. He had been reelected to his office five consecutive times and saw no reason not to be reelected another five times, which would insure him an adequate retirement. Greer was a decent enough man and had few enemies even among the drunks and pickpockets that he regularly held in his jail. He did not abuse men unless they tried to abuse him first, and his three deputies had all been chosen for their pleasantness and self-restraint from anger and excessive violence.

Sheriff Greer stood six feet tall and had silver in his hair and a perpetual grin on his wide, open face. He attended the First Baptist Church, and his wife was a favorite among the church women, while his daughter, Emily, was fifteen, pretty, and popular. The Greer family lived modestly and within their means, yet they wanted for almost nothing.

What most people did not know about Lucas Greer was

that he was totally under the control of the Ramsey family and their financial power. Very rarely did the head of the family, Amos Ramsey, ask or expect Lucas Greer to do anything outside of good moral ethics, but when Greer was asked, he was expected to toe the line.

And so now as Sheriff Lucas Greer read the telegram from Denver a second time, he felt a shiver go up and down his spine. The telegram that he held was from a United States Marshal William Vail saying that a man named Horace Ramsey from Santa Fe had been gunned down while attacking a woman also from Santa Fe, named Mrs. Rose Delamonte. And would any of the family please inform Marshal Vail concerning their wishes for burial and wire the funds necessary to meet those wishes?

"Holy god," Greer whispered to himself.

The telegraph operator, a quiet and bespectacled man named Ollie Dorman, had received and read the telegram, and his narrow face was now deeply furrowed. "It's gonna cause a real row, isn't it, Sheriff?"

"Yes, it will, Ollie. It's going to send Mr. Amos Ramsey and his family into a blood rage, and there is no telling what they'll do when I deliver this telegram."

Ollie scratched his turkey neck and said, "They'll go to Denver and kill whoever shot Horace down, and then they'll go after Mrs. Delamonte and kill her, too."

"I'm afraid you're right."

"What are you going to do about it?" Ollie asked.

"Nothing I can do except to try settle Amos down and make him think before he jumps off the deep end. Denver is way out of my jurisdiction and I can't do a thing."

Ollie was a good and decent man who attended the same church as the sheriff and his family. "Lucas, the true Christian thing would be to send a telegram back to Denver. I can do that, and you ought to tell them that Amos Ramsey most likely will be bringing some of his boys to that city with blood in his eye so they'd best be prepared for trouble."

But Sheriff Greer shook his head. "You know I can't do that, Ollie. My job is to keep the peace in Santa Fe." He pointed down at the well-worn wooden floor. "And *this* is Santa Fe."

"I know," Ollie argued, "but everyone understands that the way that the Ramsey family got the Delamonte Ranch was—"

"Careful," Sheriff Greer advised. "Ollie, be very careful what you say, or you could get on the list. And you know what happens to people who get on the Ramsey shit list, don't you?"

Ollie gulped and nodded. "I do, but the Delamontes were good people and they were—"

"Enough!" Greer snapped, instantly regretting his outburst of anger. "Just button your lip, Ollie. You know that you signed an agreement never to gossip about the telegrams you receive and send from this office. Now, you just keep that in mind and put all of this out of your thoughts."

"But, Lucas, if you don't send something back to Denver warning those people, blood will flow in Denver," Ollie said. "And that would put the stain of sin on *both* our heads."

"Better the stain of sin on our heads than the wrath of the Ramsey family," Sheriff Greer replied, folding the telegram and slipping it into his vest pocket. "I'll try to calm Amos down and talk him out of going to Denver with his sons . . . but you know that Horace meant an awful lot to the old man. Horace looked like Amos and he was the favorite."

"Maybe so, but Horace Ramsey was a—"

"Stop," Greer ordered. "Not another word from you, Ollie. Not one more word."

Ollie sighed. "It's your call, Sheriff. But if you don't send a telegram back warning Mrs. Delamonte and those Denver people, I'm gonna wash my hands of all this trouble."

"You do that, Ollie. Just keep your mouth shut and wash your hands of it. You aren't paid to worry about this kind of trouble."

"I liked Jesse and Rose and Jesse's folks, too."

"I know. We all did. And I had a look at things, and there was never any actual proof of wrongdoing. It was . . . it was just a whole lot of misery and misfortune that fell upon the Delamonte family."

"Misfortune? Oh, bosh! Someone ambushed Jesse Delamonte, and I sure don't see how you claim there was never any wrongdoing."

Lucas Greer's lips formed a hard, white line, and without saying another word he left the telegraph office and headed over to the bank to sit down and try to talk some reason into Amos Ramsey. Amos Ramsey, who owned half of the town and was trying to buy or steal the other half. Amos Ramsey, who contributed heavily to Greer's reelection campaign every two years and who expected absolute loyalty in exchange for the sheriff's biannual reelection success and yearly pay raises.

A few minutes later Sheriff Greer stepped into Santa Fe's biggest and most prosperous bank and took a deep breath. At that moment he would rather have taken a physical beating than deliver this news to Amos. But he squared his broad shoulders, put a frozen smile on his face, and in the busy bank lobby greeted people that he knew well.

"Morning, Sheriff. How is the missus today?" Mrs. Melville asked.

"Fine," he said. "Busy as a bee in a bonnet."

"She's a dear heart. And so is that daughter of yours. Emily is going to have her pick of the bachelors when she's of a mind to do it."

"Hopefully," Greer said, meaning it, "that won't be for quite some time yet."

Mrs. Melville laughed. "Well, you never know when a pretty girl will fall head over heels in love and want to get hitched."

"I'm afraid you're right," Lucas Greer said, tipping his hat to the lady as she left the bank.

He walked up to the end of the row of tellers and whispered to a young man named Ned Olsen, "I need to see Mr. Ramsey."

Olsen glanced over his shoulder. "Sheriff, I'm afraid that he's in an important meeting right now."

"This won't wait," Sheriff Greer said. "I have some very bad news for Mr. Ramsey."

"I'll go tell him," Olsen said, hurrying off to the glassed-in private office of the bank president.

Sheriff Lucas Greer saw the teller step into the meeting. Saw old Amos scowl and then start to reprimand Olsen and then saw the old man's face change expression as his bald head swiveled to stare out at Sheriff Greer, who stood waiting in the lobby wringing the brim of his Stetson in his hands.

Moments later, the meeting ended and the sheriff of Santa Fe was ushered into the bank president's office. Amos Ramsey was in his mid-seventies, with a florid face, broad shoulders, and a square, prominent jaw that always reminded the sheriff of a bulldog's when he was ready to bite.

"What's the gawdamn bad news Olsen says you have for me?"

Sheriff Greer had already decided simply to give the telegram to the old man and wait to see the fireworks. Anticipating an explosion, he closed Ramsey's door so that the old man's curses could not be heard up and down the street.

"Son of a bitch!" Ramsey howled after reading the telegram and dropping it on his desk in horror. "My . . . my Horace is dead! He's been murdered in gawdamn Denver!"

"I'm sorry, sir."

Amos Ramsey's already bloodshot eyes filled with tears, and they spilled down his ruddy cheeks. He bent his head and began to sob. It was a touching sight, and Sheriff Greer actually had a moment of sympathy for the old man, even though he knew that the dead son Horace had been rotten to the core and probably deserved to die.

Amos wept pitifully for several moments, all the while cursing, slobbering, and huffing. Then he raised his head and roughly sleeved away his tears, as his round, wrinkled face became red with infused rage. "Is this it, Lucas? Is this *all* you know about the gunning down of my oldest son?"

"Yes, sir. I thought you'd want to send a telegram back to Denver telling them how you wish the burial to be held and—"

"I'm bringing Horace home!" Amos shouted. "I'm bringing my son back here to Santa Fe, and I'll bring the head of Rose Delamonte stuffed between Horace's dead legs where it belongs!"

Sheriff Greer paled and tried to batter down the image of this crude obscenity offered to him by this hateful old man. After a moment, he was able to say, "Sir, we don't know who killed Horace. I doubt it was Mrs. Delamonte and—"

Amos surged out of his office chair roaring, "Of course Rose Delamonte is the reason Horace is dead! My son loved that red-haired bitch from the first moment he laid eyes on her, but I knew she was a Jezebel! And now, because of her, poor Horace is dead! It doesn't matter who pulled the trigger that brought my son down, Rose Delamonte is the root cause of his death!"

Lucas Greer took a backward step, until his spine was pressing hard against the door. "I think you need to just settle down for a while, sir. Just try to get a strong hold of yourself and think things out a little better before you send a telegram back to Denver."

Amos Ramsey's face turned nearly purple, and Greer actually expected the old bastard might attack him. He could, of course, restrain the banker, but it wouldn't be easy or pretty, and he knew without turning around that there was a bank full of people staring at them through the glass window.

"Sir, please sit down. Is there something in here that I can pour you that might calm your nerves? To be honest, I could use a stiff drink myself, even though it's early in the day."

Ramsey shuddered the length of his fat body and collapsed back into his chair. He sniffled and then blew heartily into his handkerchief. "Let me think about what kind of a message I will send back to Denver. Let me just sit and think for a moment, Lucas."

"Take your time. You want me to leave and then come back in a while?"

"No, gawdamn you. Just . . . just take a chair and keep your silence while I think."

"Yes, sir."

Lucas Greer sat and put on his saddest face. He tried not to remember Horace for the mean little shit he had been as a boy. How the oldest Ramsey kid had always bullied those who were smaller or weaker. How Horace had once tied a rag to the tail of a stray cat, doused it with lamp oil, and lit it with a match just to see how fast the cat could run and how far it would go before it caught completely on fire and died in flaming agony.

Yes, Lucas thought, Horace had been the worst of a violent and mean family. But if Lucas valued his job, he would act as if Horace had been saintly.

"Sheriff?"

Lucas had been staring at the toes of his boots and lost in remembering what a monster Horace had been as a boy and then even worse as a man. In truth, he had been secretly afraid of Horace from the time the kid first strapped on a six-gun.

"Yes?"

"I'm going to write out a telegram and give you money that I want wired to Denver."

"Yes, sir."

Amos Ramsey began to compose a short telegram, and when he was finished he handed it to Lucas Greer and gave him a hundred dollars cash from his wallet.

"Send the telegram back to this Marshal Vail in Denver. Wire the money and make sure that it says we expect a first-class burial for my Horace with lots of flowers and a matched pair of horses to pull the hearse to the graveyard. Say that we can't come for the funeral, but we want Horace Ramsey to have the finest marble headstone available and the nicest burial plot in their best cemetery. And that there should be words spoken over him by a man of God, and flowers, lots of flowers at his graveside."

The sheriff relaxed. Maybe Amos Ramsey was going to let this go and not seek revenge after all. "Yes, sir. That sounds just fine, although all that might cost a mite more than a hundred dollars. I expect that things cost more in Denver than here in Santa Fe."

Amos retracted his fat wallet again and counted out another hundred. "That would pay for a proper burial to the gawdamn vice president of these United States."

"I expect that it would, Mr. Ramsey. I think you're doing the right thing here. Horace is gone and no one can bring him back. You've got other fine sons and the main thing—"

"Aw, shut the shit up!" Amos bellowed. "I don't need your gawdamn advice or sympathy! What I need is *revenge*! I will not rest until I can spit on that bitch's beautiful head!"

Sheriff Lucas Greer couldn't stand to look at the old man. Eyes averted, he accepted the man's message with a shaking hand and shoved it into his pocket. "So, Mr. Ramsey, what—"

"Lucas, we're all going to Denver, so you better get your bags packed because we'll be leaving before sunset."

When Lucas Greer finally processed these words, he began to shake his head. "No, sir."

"What did you just say?" the banker demanded, eyes crimping down to slits. "What the hell did you just tell me!"

Lucas squared his shoulders, took a deep breath, and looked the banker in the eyes, saying, "Sir, I'm not leaving Santa Fe to go and kill a woman or anyone else in

Denver. I have a sworn duty to uphold the laws here and protect the populace and I'm not leaving, no matter what you say."

Amos Ramsey blinked and rose to his feet. He was much shorter than his sheriff, but every bit as imposing, and for a moment, he looked like he wanted to reach into his desk drawer, grab a derringer, and kill Lucas Greer. But when he saw how many people were in his bank and watching, he managed to get his anger under control, and he hissed, "Lucas, have you forgotten what I've done for you all these years?"

"No, sir, I have not."

"And do I need remind you that you are sheriff because my money got you reelected every two years?"

"You've never let me forget it even for a day," Lucas said, feeling anger and humiliation stir in his gut. "And I've been a good sheriff."

"You've been a dutiful sheriff!"

The man was right, but Lucas tried to think about how, if he went to Denver and killed Rose Delamonte, he would ever be able to face himself in a mirror or look into the eyes of his wife and daughter without turning them away in shame. "Sir, I know you can call a town council and have me fired by noon. But even so, I'm still not going to Denver to be a part of killing the Delamonte woman or anyone else."

For a long moment, their eyes locked in combat. Finally, Amos was the first to break eye contact and his voice grated when he said, "All right. Stay here. I don't need your help in Denver. I've got loyal sons. I'll do what needs to be done to avenge the death of my favorite boy. But when I come back, and when your next reelection rolls around, we're going to have a dead serious talk about what future you still might have in Santa Fe . . . if any."

"Yes, sir. I expected you'd say that."

"And you had better remember who holds the mortgage to your house."

"You do," Lucas Greer said.

"And you had asked if I might make you a loan so you could send that pretty young daughter of yours to a school so that she could become a nurse. I think you said that the best one was in Boston and that her education was going to cost you at least a thousand dollars."

"I said that," Lucas admitted. "Emily deserves the very best education that I can afford."

"Well," the old banker said, "you can't afford Boston, but I might be willing to loan you enough money to send her somewhere closer."

"I understand."

Amos Ramsey sneered at his sheriff. "We'll be talking, Lucas. I think that you need to be reminded of many things. But for the time being, send that telegram and get out of my sight!"

The sheriff slammed his Stetson back on top of his head and set it just right. He was seething and afraid all at the same time, and he couldn't wait to get away from this viperous old bastard. While the man was gone, Lucas would send out some inquiries about other jobs in other towns. His wife and daughter would be devastated but understanding. They wouldn't fault him because they both knew just as he knew that a man had to hold on to his honor or he wasn't a man anymore.

Chapter 8

Billy Vail leaned over Longarm's battered desk and whispered, "How is Mrs. Delamonte settling into her new accommodations?"

"She's doing just fine."

"She is an extraordinarily beautiful woman." Billy shook his head. "I feel very bad about her husband and in-laws. Do you believe everything she said about the ranch?"

"I'm inclined to believe her," Longarm answered.

"If that's true, I'm not sure what will happen."

"I might take some time off and go to Santa Fe."

Billy's brow knitted. "Why?"

"Why not?" Longarm replied. "If the local authorities in Santa Fe haven't done anything to help her up to now, I don't expect that they ever will."

"That's true," Billy said. "From what you've told me, the Ramsey family sounds like it has quite a grip on the town."

"Santa Fe has been there a long time, and I'm sure that

no one family could have that much power, but you never know."

"Well," Billy mused, "let's just see if we can survive what the lady says is coming our way."

"What's this 'we' stuff?" Longarm asked his boss with a half smile. "It's me and Rose that are the bait, not you."

Billy didn't seem to take that point well but said, "I am considering putting extra men around her in a couple of days."

"I can take care of Rose."

Billy motioned for Longarm to follow him into his office, where he could shut the door and they could speak privately. "Custis, do you *really* believe Mrs. Delamonte when she says that the whole clan of Ramsey men will come to kill her and yourself?"

"Yes."

"Damnation!" Billy said, shaking his head and taking a chair. "Maybe the best thing for you and her to do is to get out of Denver and go into hiding."

"And how is that going to do anything except put off the inevitable?"

"Well, with time we could come up with some—"

"No," Longarm interrupted. "The last thing in the world I want is to have the threat of that family coming after me. I don't want to wait a week, a month, or a year looking over my shoulder and wondering if this is the day that I'll be ambushed. I don't want that and you wouldn't want it, either."

"You're right," Billy agreed. "But we have to use our heads."

"We are using them," Longarm argued. "If this Amos Ramsey and his sons are coming for me and Rose, we need to set a trap."

"With you both as the bait?"

"Can you think of any other way?"

"No," Billy admitted. "But if this goes bad and either of you is killed, I will never forgive myself."

"None of us have the luxury of certainty. None of us know what is coming tomorrow or even in the next hour. We just have to do what is right and take our chances."

"And becoming bait is right?"

"I don't know," Longarm confessed. "I'm worried just like you. What if I am shot down in ambush and Rose is with me? What if I'm wounded and can't help Rose when they grab her and slit her throat or kill her slowly? To be honest, Billy, I've been lying awake at night worrying about that kind of thing, and I'm not getting much sleep."

Billy nodded with understanding. "I'm just accustomed to going after the enemy instead of waiting for them to come. I know that you are the same way, Custis. This waiting game *is* hard on the nerves."

"Sure it is," Longarm agreed. "But if I left for Santa Fe today, then I'd probably miss them in passing"

"True, but I have other deputies that I could assign to guard and protect her."

"Uh-uh," Longarm grunted. "I'm the one that killed Horace Ramsey, and I'm the one that is going to see this through to the end."

"Okay," Billy said, looking worried.

After work that day Longarm headed straight for the rooming house. He knew that the Ramsey men could not possibly reach Denver for another few days, even if they relayed horses. So he was determined to rest and enjoy Rose Delamonte's company as much as he could.

"Custis!"

He turned to see Lucy Crabtree hurrying up the street toward him. Longarm took a deep breath and smiled. He cared for Lucy, just not enough to be tied down to her, which is what she was after.

"Hi, Lucy."

"I thought that you'd be coming by the shop on your way home."

"I . . . uh, forgot."

"Well," Lucy said, lifting up on her toes. "I think we ought to go out and have a lovely dinner and then go by my place afterward and enjoy ourselves."

Longarm thought that sounded pretty good, but he really wanted to check in with Rose and see how she was doing. "That's a fine idea, Lucy. Tell you what. I'll just go to my room and wash up a bit and then come by your place later."

"Oh," Lucy said, "I'll come along with you since we are so close to home now."

Longarm nodded, knowing there was no way to get out of this. "Okay," he said.

Five minutes later they were climbing the stairs to his room. Aggie poked her head of her door, and when she saw Longarm with Lucy, she snorted. "Well, ain't you two just the pretty pair!"

Before Lucy or Longarm could react, Aggie slammed the door.

"What was that all about?" Lucy asked, perplexed.

"Damned if I know."

"That old woman is sort of batty, isn't she?"

"I'm afraid so," Longarm agreed. "But I just pay her my rent and pay her no mind."

"Well," Lucy said, "she's got her skirt in a twist over something."

"She's *always* upset," Longarm told Lucy.

"She doesn't seem to think much of you, Custis. You don't think that she would go crazy some night, use her manager's house key to unlock your door, and try to murder you or something else terrible, do you?"

"Nah." Longarm hurried up the stairs, hoping that Rose wouldn't hear them in the hallway and suddenly open her door. If that happened, Lucy was not going to be happy over his new neighbor. Not a bit happy.

Longarm ushered Lucy into his room and closed the door quickly. He smiled and said, "It's hot up in my office and I need to rinse myself off and change shirts."

"Take your time," Lucy told him. "My new manager is working out just fine, and I'm confident that she is taking good care of my business. But when we leave I'd like to stop by for a few minutes just to check up."

"Whatever," Longarm said, removing his hat, string tie, and shirt.

Lucy sat down on the bed and studied his bare and very scarred but muscular torso. "Sometime I'm going to count all the scars on your body."

"What for?" Longarm asked, pouring a bowl of water so that he could take a quick rinse-off.

"It's just that I've never seen so many scars on one body in my life," Lucy replied, getting up and coming over to stroke his back and study his scars more closely. "And you've got some on your butt, don't you?"

"Lucy," Longarm said feeling a bit exasperated, "can we possibly change the subject?"

She kissed his bare chest and then began to unbutton his pants. "My curiosity is aroused and I want to see how many you have below your beltline."

"I've only a few," he said, gently pushing her back.

"I think you've got three on your butt cheeks alone."

"Lucy!"

She laughed and pulled down his pants. Longarm couldn't help but start laughing, too, and then they were on the bed, tearing off their clothes, and the laughter got even louder. Longarm slapped Lucy's hands off his butt, and she grabbed his manhood and told him that she wanted to see if *it* was scarred.

"Dammit, Lucy, you know very well that it's perfect."

"You can say that again!"

Lucy started biting and kissing, and they were just about to join when, suddenly, there was a loud banging on the wall near the bed.

"Custis! Custis, what's so funny over there!"

Lucy froze, hand clenching Longarm's stone-hard pillar. "Who the hell is *that*?"

"Never mind."

"It sounded like a woman."

"Nah. Well, maybe it was. Have to check on that later." Longarm was aroused, and he wanted to ride Lucy now that they had gotten this far in their little erotic game. He tried to push her lovely thighs apart, but there it was again.

"Custis! What's going on over there! Are you all right?"

"That *is* a woman! And she's right next to us."

"She is not," he said. "She's in the next room."

Lucy rolled off the bed. "Who is 'she'?"

He made a grab for her, but she was too quick. "Just a new tenant. Lucy. Never mind."

Lucy Crabtree wasn't a woman to be put off or fooled by much, and now she rushed over to the wall and pounded on it, yelling, "Who the hell are you!"

There was silence in the next room, broken only by the groan that escaped Longarm's lips.

"Answer me!"

"I'm Rose."

"Rose who?"

A moment of silence, then, "Come to the door and let's meet."

"No," Longarm pleaded.

"Be just a minute!" Lucy snapped, grabbing her clothing and getting quickly dressed. She glared at Custis and hissed, "This Rose you have as a new neighbor had better be *real* ugly."

Longarm grabbed his pants and started pulling them on. "Listen," he said, "I was going to tell you about this woman from Santa Fe. A *widow* woman still very much in love with her poor, dead husband, but I forgot and . . ."

Lucy wasn't even listening. She got one shoe on and hobbled over to the door, already furious. She wasn't fully dressed when she tore the door open and then took a step back and stared at Rose.

"Hello," Rose said, glancing past Lucy toward Longarm, who was madly trying to buckle his pants. "I guess this probably isn't a good time for me to be introducing myself to the pair of you."

"Oh," Lucy said, ice in her voice, "I think your timing is just perfect. Come on inside for a moment."

"No!" Longarm cried.

Rose shook her head. "I just heard noises and . . . well, given our situation, I had to find out if something was wrong."

"I'm very glad that you did," Lucy said, her voice icy with anger as she glanced back at Longarm with daggers in her eyes. "And we will most certainly get better acquainted some other time. I own Lucy's Floral Shop just up the street. Please stop by and we'll have a chat."

"Thank you, I will," Rose replied, forcing her own smile, then disappearing.

"Well," Lucy said, slamming the door and putting her hands on her hips. "You want to try and explain that woman to me?"

"Would it do any good?"

"Nope. Not even a little bit."

Longarm reached for her shirt. "Lucy, her life is in danger, and my boss and I thought it would be good if I stayed close until the danger was past."

"How wonderfully convenient for you," Lucy said, sarcasm dripping from her mouth. "And I can see that this job is really going to be a hardship upon you, Custis."

Longarm wanted to tell her about how he'd shot Horace Ramsey to save Rose, but there just wasn't time. Before he could collect his words and frame his story, Lucy Crabtree grabbed the one shoe she was wearing and hurled it across the room at him, an instant before she left, slamming the door.

Longarm collapsed on his bed. "Well, that was a complete fuckin' disaster," he said to the ceiling. Even worse than he could have imagined. Now he had Lucy on the prod and a beautiful woman in the next room who was still in love with her dead husband. This was not a good situation.

Chapter 9

The next morning Longarm clomped into the office and plunked down in his chair, looking either angry or upset. He had some overdue paperwork on the desk, but when he'd idly gone through it he grabbed everything up in a pile and shoved it into a drawer.

"What's wrong?" a deputy at the nearest desk asked. "Have a lonely night for a change?"

Longarm pinned Deputy Herb Pelkey with his dark brown eyes and said, "At least *every night* isn't a lonely night for me."

Pelkey was a slab of a man, heavyset and with a walrus mustache and a big moon face. He was said to be a good shot with either a pistol or rifle, although his Boston accent and expensive clothes set him apart from most Westerners. Pelkey was always cracking jokes and trying to be the center of attention when, in fact, no one could stand the bastard. But Pelkey either couldn't see that or refused to accept the notion that anyone wouldn't be charmed by him and his bad jokes. Longarm didn't wish any ill on the man at the next desk, but he sure hoped that Pelkey either got scared, wounded, or just fed up with being a deputy United States Deputy marshal. But that was very unlikely. How the man had gotten hired continued to be an amazement and a source of much office speculation. Herb Pelkey had arrived at the Denver Federal Building from Washington, D.C., with a guaranteed job in the form of a written executive order. Billy Vail hadn't hired him or requested he be transferred into the office. But the rumor was that Pelkey had many important connections in Washington, and although everyone tried to get him to tell them who, on that single subject alone Herb Pelkey was an absolute mummy.

"Oh," Pelkey said, "I do pretty well out there with the women. They are pretty stupid and uneducated, so they're easy pickings for an educated man like me. Maybe I don't do quite as good as you, but that's only because I haven't been in Denver long enough to meet as many ladies."

"'Ladies'?" Longarm asked, eyebrows shooting up in feigned surprise. "Why I thought you were more interested in young men."

Someone in the office burst out in cackles. Pelkey's round cheeks turned crimson and he began to shake with pent-up fury. "One of these days I'm going to have to teach you a little respect. Did I ever tell you how I went sixty-seven rounds with the great fighter Irish O'Toole and fought him to a bloody draw?"

"Yeah, you told me . . . about forty times," Longarm said, getting up and starting to pace back and forth out of boredom. "And everyone else, too. Only the last time it was fifty-six rounds."

Pelkey blinked. "Well . . . I mean, we fought twice, and the second time we went sixty-seven rounds."

"Stow it, Herb. I really ain't interested in your stories this morning."

"You are an arrogant asshole, Custis and—"

Longarm pivoted around on his left boot heel and slapped Pelkey across the side of his round, red face so hard that the smaller man went over backward in his office chair. Before Pelkey could recover, Longarm kicked him in the groin, and then when Pelkey howled and sat up to cradle his testicles, Longarm smashed him in the jaw and knocked him out cold.

"Oh, shit," exclaimined Claudia, a woman who worked in the office. Looking down at Deputy Pelkey, she said, "Custis, you've really done it this time!"

"Have I, now?" He stood up and stared at the gaping faces. "Pelkey has had that coming to him since the first day he arrived, and by gawd this morning I'd just had a belly full of his bullshit."

"Good for you, Custis!" several deputies shouted.

"Do you know who Deputy Pelkey is connected to?" Claudia asked.

"I don't know and I don't much give a damn."

"The *vice president*."

"Ah, come on."

"No, seriously. He's a cousin or something to our vice president, and I'm sure that Herb will fire off a telegram to Washington, D.C., saying that you assaulted him without cause and you should be arrested and immediately terminated from federal employment."

"Send off a telegram, huh?" Longarm knelt beside the unconscious deputy and grabbed his fat fingers. "If I'm going to get fired anyway, I might as well break a few bones."

"No!" Claudia cried in horror.

"All right," Longarm said, dropping the hand. "But when this asshole wakes up, tell him I'd be more than happy to go a few rounds with him inside or outside of the ring."

"Custis!"

Longarm turned to see his boss hurrying into the room.

"What the hell is going on here!" Billy's eyes kept ricocheting back and forth between Longarm and his unconscious deputy.

Longarm just shrugged. "He lost his mind and called me an 'arrogant asshole.' Wrong thing for Herb to say."

"Well, did you provoke him?"

"Not much." Longarm shrugged. "A deputy marshal has got to learn how to control himself and what he says. It was just a long overdue lesson, Billy."

Billy knelt beside Herb Pelkey. "He's out colder'n a mackerel."

"Yeah," Longarm answered with a wide grin. "And ain't his rare silence golden!"

Billy wasn't in any mood for humor. "A couple of you men get Herb up and into his chair. Claudia, find a towel and soak it with cold water. I sure hope his jaw isn't broken."

"I doubt that it is," Longarm said, watching the commotion. "I didn't really put everything I had into the punch."

"Damn," Billy said when they dragged Pelkey's chair upright and then plopped him into it. "Herb is going to want some payback on this one, Custis. You know the man."

"No, I don't know the man, and I don't want to know the man," Longarm said. "But if he comes at me, I'll put him in the hospital, so you had better have a good talk with him about who he calls what in this office."

"Do you realize that Herb is connected to the vice president? Did you know that?"

"Nope, and it wouldn't make any difference if he was the president's favorite son. I don't like him, and he needs to go back to Washington or Boston or wherever the hell he is from."

"That, unfortunately, isn't my decision to make," Billy confessed. "Longarm, I think you and I need to have a private conversation in my office this morning."

"Got any whiskey in your drawers?"

"Follow me, Marshal Long."

"Yes, sir," Longarm said, winking at Claudia as he followed his boss through the office.

Once inside with the door closed, Billy said, "I know that no one here likes Deputy Pelkey, but—"

"Ain't any buts about it, Boss."

"But he's here and we have to deal with him."

"Send him out in the field more often," Longarm suggested as he took a chair. "The man is a cancer in this office. No one even smiles anymore. Pelkey is always runnin' off at the mouth. Today, he just said the wrong words, and now maybe he'll think about what he says before opening his fat mouth."

"I know he's trouble," Billy said. "Do you think I like having someone under me who can criticize everything I do to the vice president?"

"No, I suppose not. Send him to Santa Fe," Longarm suggested. "Tell him what is going on with the Ramsey family."

Billy blinked with surprise. "Are you serious?"

"Sure," Longarm replied. "Number one, it would get Herb out of here for a few weeks, and number two, maybe he'll stick his nose into something he can't handle and be killed. Either way, it's a big gain for all of us."

"Jesus, Custis. That's pretty hard."

"It's pretty much the way I feel about Deputy Pelkey. Send him on out to Santa Fe. Who knows? Maybe he'll even dig up something useful on the murders of Rose's husband and in-laws."

Billy frowned and doodled with his pencil. "Let me think about that."

"Better think fast, because I believe you are right about him coming after me," Longarm said. "I never killed one of our own and it's not something I'd like to do, but I will if necessary."

"Okay. Okay. I'll send Herb to Santa Fe, providing you didn't mess up his head. How many times did you hit him?"

"Slapped him across the side of the face. Kicked him in the balls, then punched him in the jaw. The slap just set his eyeballs rolling around in his fat face, the other two blows probably hurt pretty bad . . . or will hurt when they get him revived."

Billy clucked his tongue with obvious disapproval. "Custis, if the office of the vice president decides to look into this and come after you, there isn't a hell of a lot I can do to protect you and your job."

"Don't even try, Billy. You'd only get yourself in the mess. and there's no reason for both of us to wind up in shit stew."

"What about Mrs. Delamonte?"

"What about her?"

"How is she?"

"Breathing and lookin' pretty good," Longarm replied, wondering what was really on Billy's mind.

"You . . . you screwed her yet?"

Longarm guffawed. "Why, Billy. You are so delicate with your words."

"Can it, Custis. Are you screwin' her yet?"

"Not yet," he said. "Lucy Crabtree came over late yesterday and things got a little complicated. Both of the women are on the prod as far as I'm concerned."

It was finally Billy's turn to grin. "My, oh my! How about that can of tomatoes!"

"Billy, what is it you are circling around about here like buzzards on a dying dog?"

"Those Ramsey men, if they've been traveling on a train, could be arriving by tomorrow."

"I've thought about that."

"And when they arrive, I don't want you here at the office kickin' Herb's ass around the place. I want you near Mrs. Delamonte all the time."

"By that you mean day and night."

"Yep."

"So that's why you're asking if I'm bedding the woman?"

Billy cast his eyes aside for a moment. "Yes, that's why I'm asking."

Longarm leaned far back in his chair and stared at the ceiling. "Actually, Billy, I was thinking along the same lines. If someone smashed into her room, even though it is right next to mine, they could shoot her and run before I could wake up, grab my gun, and get out into the hallway."

"So what are you going to do?"

"I'm going to move in with Mrs. Delamonte," he said.

"Any indication that she'll go for that?"

"Nope. Maybe you could write an official letter saying

that she is under your department's protection twenty-four hours a day and I'm the one to do it."

"I'll do that right now."

"Thanks," Longarm said with a big smile. "It'll be like givin' a thief the keys to the home safe."

Billy looked up at his friend. "I could send you to Santa Fe, and Deputy Pelkey to live with Mrs. Delamonte until this threat to her life passes."

"Yeah, I know you could do that," Longarm said, "and you could also wind up with your head stuffed up your ass."

Billy chuckled. "You can't talk to your boss like that."

"I just did."

"Well," Billy said, "you're lucky I've got a hell of good sense of humor."

"Yeah, I am," Longarm said as Marshal Billy Vail pulled a sheet of official paper from his desk and began to write.

Chapter 10

Deputy Marshal Herb Pelkey jumped up from his chair, round face split in a wide grin. "Jesus, Chief Vail, I can't believe that you've given me the chance to *finally* do something important out of this office. I was beginning to think that—"

"Think *what*?"

"Well, that maybe I was on your shit list. I couldn't imagine why that might be, unless it's that I dress nicer than you and the others and come from a family with money back East."

Billy stared up at the man. His jaw was so swollen that even with a full-moon face, he looked goofy and out of kilter. But mostly, it was just something about this man that made other men want to either punch him or walk away shaking their heads.

"Listen," Billy said, exercising all of his considerable patience. "I've told you about the Ramsey family and about how they might come to kill Mrs. Rose Delamonte."

"Yeah, and that son of a bitch Custis Long." The shamed deputy actually smiled.

Billy managed to say. "Herb, I'm giving you this assignment on one condition."

"And that is?"

"That what happened between you and Custis Long remains in this office. And there will be no retaliation, no hard feelings on the part of either of you."

"But he sucker punched me, and when I was down he laid a boot to my balls and damn near broke my jaw!"

"Yes, and just before that you called him an 'arrogant asshole.' Not a very wise thing to do on your part."

Deputy Pelkey shook his head. "But . . ."

"No buts about this. A fight in my office, if leaked to the press, would be very bad for all of our careers."

"And you expect me to just . . . just let what he did in front of everyone pass!"

"That's right," Billy said. "That's the deal."

"I get it. You're not doing this for me, you're doing it for your special boy. The one that everyone bows to as if he walks on water."

"Herb," Billy said, his voice becoming tense. "This is strictly between you and me. I need a deputy to go to Santa Fe, New Mexico, and sniff around. Investigate the murders of the Delamontes. Telegraph me what you learn every day. Be discreet and be careful because this family is supposedly both dangerous and powerful."

Deputy Pelkey sniffed in disdain, although it was an odd sound because he couldn't open his jaws all the way. "I know what family power is all about and what *real* danger is, Chief Vail. No backwoods crackers are gonna get an edge on me in Santa Fe. I know how to talk to people with money, so you're doing the right thing by sending me instead of Custis."

"I think I am," Billy Vail said. "Now, we'll cut you a check for some travel money and . . ."

"I don't need it. I want to get on the train and get movin' today. I'll keep a record of my expenses and present them when I get back here with my reports and maybe more."

"As you please." Billy glanced at the clock and said, "I expect that you can catch the southbound Denver and Rio Grande, which will be arriving before long. After a short layover for taking on water and coal it will head south in four hours."

"I'll be traveling first class, of course."

"Herb, you know that my people travel a step lower than that to save the taxpayer money."

"I'll make up the difference with my *own* money." Pelkey stretched up to his full height and said, "I was taught that, if you travel first class, you *feel* first class. And I *am* first class!"

A first-class asshole, Billy thought to himself as the man headed out his office door.

An hour later Deputy Marshal Herb Pelkey was strutting around the loading platform waiting for the inbound to arrive. He was woman-watching, one of his favorite pastimes, but there wasn't a lot to see today. Maybe, he thought, there would be some luscious ones heading down to Pueblo that he could ogle.

When the train finally did pull into the station, Deputy Pelkey had positioned himself in a good watching place. He liked to watch people, especially young ones, girls and even boys.

One by one the passengers disembarked onto the platform. The conductor helped the ladies and kids down and almost held out his hand for tips for the better dressed men. Most of them, Pelkey noted, ignored the hand and headed for the depot.

A blond woman stepped down wearing a tight skirt and blouse and flanked by a group of men. The woman was exceptionally attractive, and she reminded Herb of an expensive whore he had favored back in Washington, D.C. In fact, the resemblance was so strong that it was arousing him. But the men that were with her were an interesting mix. One was old, rugged and looked like a prosperous rancher; the others were tough and dressed as cowboys, except their clothes were well tailored and expensive. They wore big, wide-brimmed Stetsons and high-heeled boots. The guns on their hips looked as serious as their grim expressions.

As the new arrivals collected their bags and moved past Pelkey, he overheard the woman say, "I hope we can get this over and get the hell back to Santa Fe. I already don't like the look or feel of Denver."

"We'll take as long as it takes to pay our proper respects to your Horace," the old man snapped. "He was my son and your brother, gawdammit!"

A light went on brightly in the round globe of Deputy Marshal Herb Pelkey's head. Horace. Did they say Horace and Santa Fe?

Suddenly, he was so excited he could barely see straight. These people were the Ramsey family and they were here to kill Rose Delamonte and Custis Long! The cemetery visit was just a tag-on obligation!

Deputy Pelkey was packing iron. A Colt at his side that he had practiced thousands of times using in a fast draw and thousands more target practicing at a shooting range just outside the nation's capital. And he carried a two-shot derringer in his pocket that he hoped women would see bulging there and believe meant that he was well endowed.

And now . . . now he had a handful of people that he could arrest or kill. Oh, but wait a minute here. Could he really kill all of those men before one of them killed him? And what about the woman? She'd be armed, he'd bet his sweet ass on that, and she had the look of someone who would not faint in a fight.

Deputy Pelkey eased his hand away from his gun butt as his mind worked furiously for the best solution. He should tail them, of course. Find out where they were going to stay in town and then report what he'd learned to his boss.

But then . . . if he did that . . . Chief Vail would send Custis Long and some of the other deputies to confront these Ramsey people and he would get nothing. Nothing!

"To hell with that," Pelkey said as he fell about fifty feet behind the new arrivals. "I'll play this out awhile and figure out my best move."

He followed the group to the Hotel Vanderbilt, one of the nicest in town, and stood just outside the lobby glancing at them as they registered and had their bags taken up to their rooms. All of them were ushered into what Herb knew was the hotel's elegant dining room.

Gawd but that woman was good-looking! How he would like to . . .

Deputy Pelkey swallowed hard when, a moment later, the woman exited the dining room and entered the lobby alone. She spoke to the hotel's desk clerk and then seemed a little unsure what to do before she sat in a big leather sofa chair and found a magazine.

This is my chance! Pelkey thought. This is my best chance to work this to my sole advantage!

He polished one of his expensive boots on the back of each trouser leg, removed his hat and slicked his hair, then glanced at his reflection in the window. That sonofabitchin' Custis Long! Pelkey gently rubbed his massively swollen jaw and tried to force an expression that diminished the unsightly effect, but he gave up and decided that he would just have to proceed as if he were looking his normal handsome self.

Do it! he thought. She's beautiful but just an ignorant ranch girl from New Mexico. Probably stupid and uneducated. Don't show her your badge or tell her you are a federal marshal. Not at first. She'll be impressed by the cut of your clothes, your big words, your smooth confidence and superior breeding. She will admire and then maybe even want you tonight. Do it now!

He pushed inside the elegant lobby and strolled confidently toward the beautiful blonde from Santa Fe, New Mexico. Deputy Pelkey pasted a wide smile on his lopsided face and peered down at her loveliness.

"Good morning, miss," he said, removing his hat.

She glanced up, then dismissed him by turning back to her magazine.

"Excuse me," Pelkey persisted.

"Whoever you are and no matter what you are selling, get out of my sight."

Pelkey cleared his throat and revised his plans. "I don't think that would be in your best interest or that of your . . . companions from Santa Fe."

Her head snapped up and the magazine fell from her hands.

Now he had her full attention!

She reached into her handbag and found her own deadly derringer. Without rising, she asked, "Who are you and what do you want?"

"I want to help you *and* help myself. May we talk privately?"

"No one can overhear us unless we shout. And we're not going to shout, are we?"

"No," Pelkey promised, "we are not."

"How do you know we came in from Santa Fe?"

He pulled out a first-class ticket. "I was on the way there myself and standing on the platform. I happened to overhear you and your friends as you passed."

"They aren't my friends. They are my family. What do you want?"

"I want fame and fortune, like most. I want a man named Marshal Custis Long dead or crippled . . . as I suspect you and your 'family' do."

She looked intently into his eyes. "Just who the hell are you?"

He decided to make his big move. Easing his badge out of his pocket, he showed it to her and her alone.

For a moment, she froze, as if in indecision, then she said, "You show me that badge and then tell me you want a Marshal Custis Long *dead*?"

"He did this to my jaw." No use in telling her that his balls were purple and big enough to put a stud horse to shame.

A small trace of a smile appeared at the corners of her lovely lips. "I see."

"Son of a bitch sucker punched me, knowing I'd beat the hell out of him in a fair fight."

"And *that's* why you want him dead?"

"That and other reasons that are private. Do you want

to talk about serious things? The federal marshal's office is expecting you people."

Etta Ramsey took a deep breath. "I want to talk to you, Officer, but I really can't."

Herb blinked. "Why not? Would you like to find a room and—"

"No," she said quickly. "I can't talk without my family around me. This concerns *all* of our lives, does it not?"

He had to nod his head. "It does."

"Then I'll go into the dining room and tell them about you. What is your name?"

"I'd rather not say right now," Pelkey said, trying to figure out exactly when he had lost control of this conversation. "But . . ."

"Meet us here this evening."

"No. Too public."

"Then come up to our rooms."

Pelkey found himself shaking his head because that seemed way too dangerous.

"All right," she said, "then where can we talk in private?"

"The train depot. There will be a ticket agent and telegraph operator on duty. We can stand on the platform and talk. No one will be around except those two."

"Fine," she said, rising to leave.

Deputy Pelkey lowered his voice. "Are you married?"

"No. Are you?"

"No."

She gave him a smile to melt any man's cold heart. "Then tonight."

"There will be witnesses inside the train depot, but they won't be able to overhear a word we say," he reminded her, suddenly worried about this meeting. And how would he explain to Billy Vail the reason why he didn't take the train out of town today?

Deputy Pelkey decided that he'd miss the train and hole up until dark. Hole up and then wait and see what he could do to get revenge and make himself famous in one night, and maybe even . . . maybe even end up humping the beautiful Etta Ramsey.

Chapter 11

Longarm knocked on Rose Delamonte's door, but there was no answer. He knocked louder, but still no answer.

"Damn!" he swore. Didn't she know that the Ramsey men could be here as early as today?

He debated going down to his landlady and asking the old battle-ax for a key to Rose's room . . . but rejected the idea. Aggie would refuse his request and then give him hell for even thinking about getting a lady's room key.

So what to do now?

Longarm decided that he would go look for Rose, because, after all, she couldn't have wandered too far away in a big, strange city.

When he got to the street, he looked left then right, and chose the latter direction. A few minutes later, as he passed Lucy Crabtree's floral shop, he glanced through the window and saw Lucy and Rose nose-to-nose in deep conversation.

"Uh-oh," he said, ducking aside. "This can't be a bit good for me."

Longarm lit a cigar and smoked it impatiently, and when Rose finally emerged from the shop, he followed her a block and then caught up, saying, "Good afternoon. I've been looking everywhere for you."

Rose turned on him and her expression wasn't friendly. "Oh, yeah?"

"Yeah."

"Well, you might as well know that I was just talking to Miss Crabtree and she had *lots* to say about you."

Longarm squirmed. "You can't believe everything Lucy tells you. She tends to . . . uh, exaggerate."

"I don't think she exaggerated at all when she said that you two were talking about marriage."

Longarm's reaction was to step back and hold up both hands in self-defense. "Whoa! I never talked to her about getting married."

"That's not what Miss Crabtree says."

"Okay. Okay," Longarm said. "Lucy would like us to get married, but I never told her that we would. In fact, I was very honest with her and said that I'm never going to be the marrying kind."

"Footloose and fancy free, huh?"

"Well, in a manner of speaking I suppose that I am."

"Yes, I'm beginning to understand exactly what kind of a man you are, Marshal Long."

"Listen, I'm not the rogue or villain here. I am as giving as I am receiving. Lucy just never would stop talking about marriage, which is the reason that I was going to end the affair."

Rose started walking swiftly toward their rooming house. "Well, don't you even think of ending it on my account, because after talking to that poor woman, I really don't want anything to do with you!"

"She's not poor. Lucy is loaded! She could have most any man she wants in this town."

"And I'm sure that she will," Rose snapped.

Longarm hurried after her. "Rose, my boss and I have decided that the Ramsey people could arrive at any time and that your life is in serious danger starting today."

"Tell me something I didn't already know."

"All right," Longarm said, trotting around to block her path. "I need to room with you."

"What!" she cried so loudly that other passersby stared.

"You heard me."

"If you think that I can't guess what you really have in mind, then you are clueless."

"It's not that!"

She put her hands on her hips. "Oh? It's not that you think this would put you in my bed and in my . . . my body?"

"No! I need to be close all the time in order to protect you."

"And who, might I ask, would protect me from *you*?"

Longarm couldn't answer that one, so he said, "Rose, I could drag my mattress and blankets into your room . . . you've already furnished it nicer than mine . . . and I'd be willing to sleep on your floor. Or you could sleep in my bed and I'd sleep on the floor there. Either way, you'd be a lot safer."

"Get that thought completely out of your thick head, you big lunk! I'm not going to 'room' with you or any other man. I'm still a married woman."

"You're a widow, Rose."

Tears welled up in her eyes and she hurried on. Longarm just followed her, feeling rather rotten inside. But dammit, he and Billy were right, Rose Delamonte should not be left alone . . . even at night.

Especially at night.

"We sent a telegram to Santa Fe, but the authorities there haven't sent anything back. Doesn't that strike you as a bad sign?"

"It's what I expected," Rose told him. "The sheriff is a man named Lucas Greer. He's a personable fellow, but he's like a dog on Amos Ramsey's leash. Same goes for the town deputies under Greer. I could have told you that you wouldn't hear anything back from them."

"We're sending a deputy to Santa Fe to investigate things."

"He'll be a dead deputy before the month is over," Rose predicted.

Longarm thought of Deputy Herb Pelkey and figured that Rose was probably right about what would be the outcome in Santa Fe.

"Rose, I'll give you my word of honor that I won't touch you."

"If we're in separate rooms, you can't touch me anyway."

Longarm had never seen such a stubborn woman. "I'm going to do what I have to do to save your life whether you like it or not."

Rose stopped at the stairs that lead up to their rooms. "All right," she told him. "You can stay with me in my room at night. But not all day. Frankly, if I didn't drive you crazy, then you'd drive me crazy if we were around each other that much."

"Okay," he agreed. "But when you leave the building like today, I'm going to tag along. Have we got a deal?"

"We have. Now, would you like to get us a good bottle of wine and join me in my room for a drink before dinner?"

Two bottles, Longarm thought with a nod and a smile, and she'll melt in my arms and I'll teach her some real lovemaking.

Chapter 12

Deputy United States Marshal Herb Pelkey was pacing rapidly up and down the deserted train station platform when Etta and what he supposed were two of her brothers appeared as if out of a grave. Pelkey felt a cold chill pass up and down his spine, but he was as fast as any man with a gun and he stood squarely in the lamplight so that the two railroad employees could see him.

Etta Ramsey looked composed and even had a smile on her pretty face when she stopped and said, "Good evening, Marshal Pelkey. These are my brothers."

"Nice to meet you," Pelkey said, extending his hand, which was ignored. "Well then, if that is how this is going to go, we might as well get right down to the purpose of this meeting."

"Yes," Etta said, "do tell us the purpose of this meeting because, quite frankly, we don't understand what any of this is about."

"I think you do," Pelkey said. "Marshal Custis Long, a man that I very much dislike and have to work next to in the office, shot and killed your brother Horace in cold blood. Your brother was lured to a lonely spot near Cherry Creek by a woman that you well know . . . Mrs. Rose Delamonte . . . and then Horace was gunned down like a dog."

Etta's smile died. "That is what we heard, too. But perhaps we have only come to collect our dear fallen brother's remains and take them back to Santa Fe. Nothing illegal about that, is there?"

"No," Pelkey said, "if it were true. But Rose Delamonte has told our department that you not only had her in-laws killed in something that was made to look like an accident, but that you had her own husband shot down in ambush."

"She's a lyin' bitch!" one of the brothers spat. "We didn't do anything to her or her kinfolk. The sheriff in Santa Fe cleared us of any connection to those deaths."

"Ah, yes, a man named Sheriff Lucas Greer."

"That's right. How'd you know?"

Pelkey smirked. "We're a big city here and I'm a federal officer, not some yokel carrying a tin star in some one-horse town."

"You wired Santa Fe," Etta said. "You wired to find out about us."

"That's right."

"And what did you hear back from Sheriff Greer?"

Pelkey's smirk faded. "Actually, nothing. I was supposed to be on the train out of here today and to go to Santa Fe and investigate the accusations made by Mrs. Delamonte."

"You can investigate until the sun falls from the sky," the other brother said with a chuckle that had no warmth, "but you won't find any connection between us and those deaths."

"I might and I might not," Pelkey replied. "I should tell you right here and now that I have very high connections in Washington, D.C. And, if anything . . . anything bad at all . . . should befall me, then the vice president himself would send more lawmen than you could possibly imagine and the truth would be known."

"Is that a threat?" Etta Ramsey asked.

"No. Just a fact," Pelkey said, eyes darting back and forth between them.

Etta pursed her lips. "What is it that you *really* want, Marshal? Money or revenge or fame?"

"All three," Herb Pelkey said quickly. "I'm an ambitious man."

"So it would seem."

One of the brothers removed a cigar and lit it without offering Pelkey one. He blew smoke just over the marshal's head and drawled, "You got a plan in mind?"

"No," Pelkey told him. "I only want you to kill Marshal Custis Long."

"And what about Mrs. Delamonte?" Etta asked. "Do you want us to kill her, too?"

"If she's the reason for your brother's blood being spilled, then I'll leave that decision to you and your family."

"Where are they?"

Pelkey told them the address and even gave them directions. He ended up with a warning. "Marshal Custis Long is very, very dangerous. He's killed a lot of tough men and he is expecting something."

"Thanks for the warning," one of the brothers said. "But we can handle him."

"I'm sure you can, but don't underestimate Custis Long. If you bust into his room, then by the time you break down the door he'll have a gun in his hand and he'll kill you. Maybe all of you."

"You make him sound real, real bad," another brother said, not sounding at all worried. "But what about you?"

Herb Pelkey felt sweat erupt from his scalp, and he had to struggle to keep his voice calm and level. "I'm going to Santa Fe like I've been ordered. Of course I'll talk to Sheriff Greer and his deputies. Then, I'll come to the same conclusion as everyone else, that there was no wrongdoing. I understand that you were able to obtain ownership of the Delamonte ranch."

"What of it?" Etta demanded.

"Probably worth some real money. I was thinking that given that I'm going to be the federal officer who gives your family the final clean slate . . . well, I ought to be rewarded."

"How much?" the taller of the tall brothers hissed.

"Ten thousand dollars. Five now, five when I file my report, which will be a public record."

The three exchanged glances, then Etta said, "You are very well dressed, Marshal Pelkey."

"Thank you."

"You don't look like the kind of man that is short of money, and you do have those Washington, D.C., connections with the vice president's office."

"That's right."

"So why should we pay you in addition to taking care of the man that obviously kicked your ass and humiliated you?" a brother asked.

Herb Pelkey felt heat rising into his cheeks. One of the brothers towered over him, and his throat suddenly constricted, so that when he spoke, his words sounded strange even in his own ears. "No one has enough money. And if you pay me, then I'll have some proof that you are all very much grateful for my assistance in taking care of everything both here and in Santa Fe."

"We don't have that much cash here with us," Etta told him. "Not nearly."

"How much do you have to give me now?"

Etta looked at her brothers, who both slowly reached into their coat pockets and extracted their wallets. They removed all of their cash and handed it to Pelkey, one saying, "Probably about a thousand there for starters."

"Wire your bank tomorrow and tell them to have a cashier's check ready for me when I arrive in Santa Fe."

"All right," Etta said, glancing through the depot window at the two clerks who were watching them. "Are we finished here?"

"Yes," Pelkey said, "unless you would like me to show you this town."

Etta laughed outright. "Marshal Pelkey, I have to hand it to you . . . you have big brass balls."

He giggled nervously and wanted to tell her that he would like to show her his balls, but the brothers were so intimidating that he decided that would not be a wise thing to do here and now.

Herb Pelkey pocketed the cash and backed away from the trio. "I'll bid you all a good night. I fully expect not to see you again and will be on tomorrow's train when Custis Long meets his just reward and is sent straight to hell."

"Good enough," Etta said.

"And you won't forget to wire your banker in Santa Fe."

"No," Etta promised. "My father will do that tomorrow."

"Why didn't he come with you this evening?" Pelkey had to ask.

"My father doesn't like to deal with shit," Etta said with a smile. "So he sent us to do it."

Herb Pelkey's eyes blinked and his cheeks shook with fury. But when he looked into Etta's eyes, which he had earlier thought so lovely, he saw his own gravestone, and so he turned and hurried off into the night.

"Etta," one of the brothers said. "What do you think Pa will want done to him?"

"I expect that he'll tell Sheriff Greer to let him do his investigation and send the report back here or to Washington, D.C., and then I think Pa will make sure that Marshal Pelkey never returns to Denver.

The two brothers nodded with understanding and grim approval. One of them said, "That little bastard was sure hot to have you tonight, Etta."

"I know. I fully expect he'll go back to his hole and whip his meat all night. Or find some whore to blow his horn and wet his little dick."

The brothers laughed and so did Etta. But the laughter was as cold as the lingering mantle of snow still resting on the top of Pikes Peak.

Chapter 13

Longarm and Rose sat across from each other in her room after eating a wonderful pork roast that Rose had cooked with potatoes, carrots, and small, delicious onions in the downstairs kitchen. They'd had apple pie for dessert, and now the hour was growing late and they were sipping a little brandy that Longarm had brought over from his room, while Charlie the cat lay curled up and purring on Rose's lap.

"That cat really likes you," Longarm said.

"I think that Charlie likes anyone who will pet, hold, and feed him. I believe that he's still a young cat."

"I believe you are right," Longarm said. "Did you have house cats back in Santa Fe?"

"No," Rose answered. "But when I leave here, I'm going to ask our landlady, Agnes, if I can take this one back to New Mexico, unless you want him for yourself."

Longarm studied the rather ordinary but affectionate orange tabby and shook his head. "Charlie and I get along fine, but he knows I'm not his permanent meal ticket. And

I'm sure that Agnes will let you take Charlie with you. She does not like cats or dogs. She has a garden out in the back, and that's where all the local alley cats, including Charlie, love to crap, fight, and fornicate. Sometimes at night you can hear them howling and carrying on louder than the saloon boys when they're on a rip-snorting toot."

"I hope that Charlie is a good mouser because we've a lot of those in the hay barn. He'll be happier out on a ranch, but he won't have a garden to soil. We've only lived together a few days, but I already feel a strong attachment to this big cat." She took a deep breath and blinked back tears. "You see, Charlie is now all the family I have left."

"That will change in time, Rose. You're too pretty to stay unattached for very long."

"I'm not ready for another love yet."

"Things change with time."

"Did you ever lose someone you loved deeply?"

"Yes," Longarm told her, choosing not to elaborate. "You know, Rose, I'm not sure how this is going to work out. First we have to see if they've come to kill us in Denver. If we survive that, then we need to go to Santa Fe and get things straightened out once and for all concerning your late husband and his family."

"Yes, and my ranch."

"Of course."

Rose tried to brighten the conversation. "Maybe Marshal Pelkey will come up with some proof of fraud and foul play, and we can send some of the Ramsey men to prison. If that happened to Amos, he'd probably die of a heart attack before he allowed anyone to put him behind bars."

"I hope that Pelkey does come up with some hard evidence against the family," Longarm replied, very much doubting it would happen.

"Either way," Rose said, "I'm going to somehow get the ranch back, and there is that buried gold."

"Yes," Longarm said, "there is that."

She studied him closely. "I'll give you half of it if you help in the recovery of it and the ranch."

"I'll give that some serious thought."

"Do that," she urged. "There is enough buried gold on my ranch to allow you to start a new and better life. You could buy a small ranch, and I know a few good ones that are for sale. Cattle prices are way down this year because we're in a drought, and good ranches are going for a song out in New Mexico and Arizona."

Longarm grinned. "I don't suppose that any of them adjoin your ranch?"

"Actually, one of them does."

"That would be the only draw for me," Longarm said. "I'm really not cut out to be a cattleman or a cowboy."

"You just never know, Custis."

"Oh, I *do* know," Longarm said with conviction. "I admire those kinds of men, but I've never understood the fascination they have about cows. I mean, a cowman will talk your leg off about cows but what's so interesting about those big, dumb animals?"

Rose giggled. "Maybe you're really not the stuff of which cowboys and ranchers are made. How do you feel about horses?"

"I find them smarter and more interesting than cattle," Longarm replied. "However, a conversation with a horse can quickly get boring."

"I give up on you, Custis. You are just never going to be a cattleman."

"I told you that already."

"But as for horses," she said, eyes lighting up, "there is

where my real passion lies. And before I lost the ranch to Amos Ramsey, I had some pretty fine ranch horses. They had a lot of personality and cow savvy. But maybe you'd better remain a federal officer of the law after all."

"I'm not half bad at it, Rose. But there are times when I wish I were . . ."

When Longarm couldn't finish, she asked, "Were *what*?"

"*Rooted*," he declared, finally coming up with exactly the right word to describe his innermost feelings. "In my travels I've seen a lot of marriages, some in the cities, some out in country, but I have to say that most of the ones I've seen are unhappy."

"Mine wasn't."

"I know that. And when I find the occasional marriage that is really good and happy like yours must have been, I have to say that I'm downright envious."

"And you think that a happy marriage will never be in the cards for you?"

"Nope."

"Why is that?"

"I'm just too stubborn and set in my ways to make a wife happy. I'm not ready to live a life that requires daily compromises. And the other thing is that what I do is dangerous. Real dangerous at times. If I took a wife, I'd always be worrying about staying alive, and when you worry about that too much, you get overly cautious and can't do your job."

"Then stay a bachelor," she advised.

"That's my plan, and that's why Lucy Crabtree was so unhappy with me holding her off on the marriage issue," Longarm said as he arose from his chair and yawned. "What about our sleeping arrangements?"

"You're way too tall to sleep on the couch, so you can take the bed and I'll take the couch. How is that?"

"Sounds like a bad deal for you and a great deal for me."

"I'll sleep all right," Rose assured him. "How long do you think this is going to have to go on with us holed up here?"

"I'd say that if the Ramsey men don't come for us within a week, we'd better think of going to find them in New Mexico."

"They *will* come to Denver."

"Care to guess how many?"

Rose thought about that a moment then said, "Amos will come, and he'll probably bring at least two of his sons and maybe a gunhand. He also has a daughter named Etta. She's about my age, but she is as hard as nails and as dangerous as a sidewinder."

"Ugly?"

"No," Rose answered. "Etta is very attractive. She's also extremely seductive."

Longarm yawned again. "I haven't slept well lately. Think I'll hit the bed and get some sleep. The door is locked, and I'm going to shove that heavy chair in front of it. We should be fine since we're on the second story."

Rose drained her brandy glass. "From what I have learned about the Ramsey men, they'll come at us fast and in force."

Longarm had brought a double-barreled shotgun from his room, and it was loaded and ready to fire. In addition, he had two pistols and a knife. "If they come to bust down the door, all that I need is the time it takes to grab that big shotgun. You would be amazed at how a scattergun firing both barrels of fire and lead can clear a room and turn the bravest or wildest drunks into shivering cowards . . . if they survive."

"Give me the loan of one of your pistols," Rose suggested. "I have a derringer, but I'd rather have a Colt revolver."

Longarm handed her his backup pistol. "It's ready to fire."

They said good night then and Longarm went to the bed in the corner. "Good night, Rose."

"Goodnight," she replied as she gathered extra blankets and went to the couch. She regarded it for a moment, then spread her blankets on the floor near the small table. She lay down, and Charlie the cat came over and immediately curled up beside her face, purring.

"Charlie," she whispered, "if they come busting in here tonight with guns blazing, I want you to dive under the bed or the couch and stay quiet in hiding until it's over. Do you understand?"

Charlie either didn't understand or didn't care, because he stretched and then curled up and fell asleep.

Chapter 14

An hour before dawn three heavily armed men crept up the stairs and stopped right outside of Longarm's room, each taking turns striking matches in their hands. They had already figured out that that the door would be locked, probably with a deadbolt in addition to the door lock. Still, they had wanted to see the layout of the second floor so that they could better understand what they were up against.

Amos Ramsey had told them that the famed federal marshal was a very dangerous man, and the trio understood that no man is ever more dangerous than when he is cornered.

"Two locks at least. Solid hinges, solid pine door," the tallest brother whispered, turning the knob slowly and then gently putting the weight of his broad shoulder against the door. "Ain't no way we're going to bust this down in a hurry."

"No surprise there. I wonder if they're both inside."

"Most likely."

"Let's go," the youngest of the brothers said as his

match burned out and scorched his fingers, suddenly leaving the trio in pitch-black darkness.

The three men then tiptoed back down the dark hallway, then down the stairs and out into the empty street. The moon was full and there were gas lamps, so that visibility was excellent.

"I think we should just wait," the tallest and biggest of the trio said. "I could go over there by that corner, and you two could find good hiding places with a clear firing line to the front door."

The man from Texas with the pearl-handled Colt on his hip asked, "What if they stay up there and don't come out this morning?"

The smallest of the three was Alex Ramsey, and he said, "Then I think we just keep waiting until they do. We can spell each other. Always keep two of us ready while one goes off to get something to eat, take a shit. We wait until the marshal and the woman come out of the building and then we close in from at least two sides. Rose can spot and recognize us. We have to keep our hats pulled down low and don't allow her to see our faces until we're right on top of them."

"I don't like this much," the big man said, not bothering to hide his worry. "We're in a strange city and there will be a lot of people out here in a few hours."

"You got any better ideas?" the gunman from Texas asked.

Alex Ramsey had always been recognized as the smartest of the sons, while the tallest and oldest, Sam, was known for his wild temper and lack of good sense. "Look," Alex said, speaking quietly, "what if we killed them on the ground floor *inside* of the building? That way no one outside would see us."

Tex was of medium height and rather good-looking in a rakish sort of way. He dressed like a gambler and wore a pearl-handled pistol, and affixed to his fancy tied-down holster there was a big lone star. Tex was a hired gunman who had displayed his skill with a six-gun by shooting four tiny finches on the wing in the space of three seconds. After witnessing such remarkable shooting, the Ramsey men had shaken their heads in amazement and admiration.

"Tex, what do you think about what Alex said?" Sam asked, heavy brow furrowed with worry.

"Actually, Sam, it makes sense. How many rooms are on the bottom floor?"

"Got to be the same number as are upstairs," Alex told them with a shake of his head to let them know they were pretty stupid compared to himself. "So there will be four."

The men exchanged glances and then Tex pulled out his silver pocket watch and said, "It's a little after five o'clock. We passed a little café up the street that was open all night. Why don't we eat a good breakfast and be back here by six?"

"Not sure I'm going to be able to eat knowing we're going to be killing a federal marshal and a pretty woman," Alex replied. "And the whiskey I drank a while ago is still at work in my head."

"All the more reason to eat," Tex countered. "Because once we kill them, we're going to be on the move, and we won't stop moving until we're clear of this town. Besides, when you get hungry, your hand becomes unsteady and your aim is affected. Boys, trust me when I say we ought to take the next hour to eat a good, solid breakfast."

"But what if the marshal and the woman get out of bed and leave early?" Sam Ramsey wanted to know.

"Hell, would *you* leave Rose Delamonte's bed early?" Tex asked with a smile.

Sam shook his head and grabbed his crotch. "If *I* was the one in Rose's bed tonight, I'd be hammerin' her the minute I woke up, and I'd keep at 'er until I was limp as a wet weed and weak-legged."

All three men laughed out their tension, and Tex complained, "Boys, it's a damn shame we have to put a woman like that down for good."

"Maybe we could just knock her out and screw her awhile in her room," Sam eagerly suggested.

"No," Alex said. "We're killing a federal marshal, and that's going to bring the hounds of hell down on us. We can't be screwin' that woman and fartin' around. People in the building are going to hear gunshots. That place will be like a beehive in minutes."

"You're right, Alex." Tex slapped the young man on the shoulder. "Let's go get something to eat. Time is wasting and my stomach is growling, and it knows it might be a long time before it gets fed after this morning's killing is done."

The three men turned under the lamplight and headed down the street. Alex was scared but determined not to show it. The idea of having a breakfast right now made his stomach queasy. Sam, being the biggest and tallest, strode down the street looking at the quiet predawn city and thinking that it was going to be real special killing a federal marshal, the very one that had gunned down poor Horace. He'd never killed a federal marshal before . . . but then he'd never killed a woman, either. Beat a lot of them up, but that was a whole lot different from killing one. He wondered how that would feel, watching Rose Delamonte bleed out. He wondered if he might rip her dress apart and take her as she was dying.

Tex was thinking of a good breakfast. He was a little annoyed that he hadn't come up with the idea of busting into the place and then hiding in wait until the marshal and Rose came down the stairs. Hell, they could rest easy in the room with the door only a little ajar and just have it easy while they waited. They'd hear the heavy footsteps of the marshal when he came downstairs. They said that Marshal Custis Long was a big, big man. That he was broad in the shoulders, tall and powerful. Tex liked to kill men bigger than himself. And he'd already killed two whores. Rose Delamonte was a married woman sleeping with the big federal marshal. So she wasn't any different from any other whore. At least, that's the way that Tex had it figured.

"Let's have steaks, eggs, and potatoes for breakfast. Coffee, too. Let's eat like we were the man having his last meal instead of the ones that are going to do the killing."

"I wish we had a shotgun." Alex fretted as he followed Tex and Sam into the empty café.

"Mornin', gentleman!" the man with the dirty white apron said. "First customers of the day! How about some fresh coffee?"

"Sounds good," Tex said. "We'd like beefsteaks, pota-toes, and eggs. Maybe some biscuits and honey if you have 'em."

"Oh, I have all that. Meals that big will cost you a dol-lar each . . . which includes the coffee."

"Pay the man," Tex said, taking his seat at the table. "Time is a-wastin' here."

Alex had money and he paid. The coffee came, and it

was strong and good, but it didn't help settle Alex's bad stomach. He stared out through the dirty front window of the café and wished that they weren't going to have to kill a federal marshal and a beautiful woman they'd already robbed of her family and her ranch. But life was about the winnings going to the strong over the weak. The Ramsey men weren't weak, and he was not going to be the god-damn exception.

"They *both* are responsible for killing Horace," Alex said out of the blue. "The marshal pulled the trigger, but it was Rose that drove our brother into the grave."

"That's right," Tex agreed. "Kid, that's exactly what you need to be thinking this morning."

"I'm still thinking I'd like to get a good taste of that Delamonte bitch," Sam told them.

"Well," Tex said with exasperation, "you just damn can't! Listen to your kid brother when he tells us that all hell is going to break loose when we kill the marshal and the woman. And, boys, we want to be a long way from that rooming house when the law comes swarming all over this area."

"Amen," Alex said. "Sam, just quit thinking about humping Rose and start thinking about how we're going to get this job done and get back to Santa Fe. Santa Fe, where you know the whores and can have your fill of 'em."

Sam nodded. "You're right as usual. But it's gonna be such a waste of a fine flesh."

"Hey!" the cook yelled from the kitchen. "How do you boys like your steaks?"

"Bloody!" Tex shouted.

"Make that three bloody steaks," Sam yelled.

"Then they'll be right up!" the cook promised.

"What time is it?" Alex asked.

Tex extracted his fine pocket watch and consulted it. "Five-twenty-five."

"We're gonna have to eat fast," Alex said, still fretting. "And I'm still not feeling like I can eat."

"You *will* eat," Tex commanded. "And you will do your part in this, and everything will be just fine."

"I sure hope so."

Tex leaned across the table and put his face up close to that of the young and obviously anxious man. "Kid, you got brains and you got balls. You're your pa's favorite and he's counting on you pullin' your weight here this morning."

"I know. Don't worry about me," Alex said, eyes darting nervously back and forth between Tex and his big brother. "I'll be fine."

"Damn right you will," Sam Ramsey growled. "Because you may be the runt of the family, but you're still a gaw-damn Ramsey man."

Alex swallowed hard. He didn't like being called a "runt," but compared to his big brother that was what he was. Well, he might be small, but when it came time to kill Marshal Long and Rose Delamonte, his bullet was going to be as big as their bullets, and he'd plaster a grin on his face so that never again would anyone question his size or his heart.

Never again!

Chapter 15

The three men entered the small foyer on the ground floor of the rooming house and began their silent vigil. Sam, Alex, and Tex had agreed that the moment someone on the ground floor opened a door to get the mail, put out the dog or cat, or just to head off to work, they'd grab that person and shove him or her back into the room. They'd whip their hostage unconscious with a pistol, and then because they could not afford any witnesses, they'd cut their victim's throat. That accomplished, all they'd have to do is wait and listen for people coming down the stairs. Sooner or later the marshal and Rose Delamonte would appear, and just when they opened the door to leave the building, they'd be sitting ducks to attack from behind.

"If we can get to their throats without having to fire a shot, then we can drag them into the room and leave three dead people who can never identify us as their assassins," Tex reasoned. "Sam, you're the biggest, so you have your knife ready to rip out the marshal's throat. Alex, can you grab and quickly silence the woman?"

Alex really didn't want to silence the woman with a slash of his knife to her throat. The very thought of it made his stomach lurch, and he felt a moment of dizziness.

"Alex?" Sam asked, glaring at his kid brother. "Did you hear what Tex said?"

"I heard him," Alex replied. "But I never expected that I'd be the one that was supposed to kill Rose Delamonte."

"You got a problem?" Tex demanded. "Because if you have a problem, you had better tell us about it right now."

"Why don't *you* kill Rose?" Alex spat. "You're the hired assassin."

"Jesus," Tex whispered, "keep your voice down! All right, I'll cut her throat if you're not man enough to do the dirty work."

Alex was good with a gun and he was no coward. He'd been picked on and teased by his older and bigger brothers since as long as he could remember, and although he only stood five-foot, nine-inches, he was a real scrapper in a fight. And right now what he wanted to do most was to bury his fist into Tex's crotch, watch him double over in agony, and then smash him behind the ear and lay the son of a bitch out cold. Boy would that ever be impressive to his father, Sam, and everyone else at their ranch in New Mexico. Only problem with that was that if he didn't kill Tex, sooner or later the man would find a way to get back at him.

Sam studied his kid brother. "Alex, dammit, are you gonna be able to hold up your end?"

"I'll hold it up," Alex vowed. "But since Tex is getting paid to kill, let him do the woman."

"Fine," Texas growled. "At least I know where we all stand. I'll do the woman and Sam will kill the marshal one way or the other. Kid, you just step aside and have your gun in your hand as a backup."

"Okay," Alex said, not even bothering to hide his huge relief.

Sam pulled out his sack of tobacco and paper, but Tex said, "Be better if you didn't smoke until we're out of this building."

"And why the hell is that?" Sam demanded.

"If someone opens their door here and smells tobacco, they might do something unexpected. If they slammed their door shut before we could grab and kill them, then we'd be in a bad fix."

Sam wasn't bright, but even he could see that logic, so he put the makings back into his shirt pocket and leaned against the wall to wait for the first person to appear. He hoped it would be soon. It was already starting to get light outside, and he had a splitting headache from the whiskey he'd drunk hours earlier.

"What time is it?" Alex asked after a while.

Tex consulted his pocket watch. "A quarter past seven. Someone should be leaving their damned room at any minute."

"What if someone from upstairs comes down first?" Alex asked. "What if it's the federal marshal?"

"If he comes down first, I shoot him then we rush upstairs and kill the woman and run for it," Tex said. "It won't be as easy, but it'll work."

Alex nodded in agreement. He raised his hand to wipe his face and saw a tremor in his fingers. He could use a couple shots of whiskey right now, but he understood that was out of the question.

Suddenly, they heard the door lock nearest them turn. They all tensed, and when an old woman in a nightgown opened her door to take out her garbage, all three of them jumped forward and slammed her back inside. The woman screamed like a banshee and showed more strength than seemed possible as she grabbed a lamp and hurled it straight into Sam's face.

Tex went at her with a knife. He clamped his hand over her screaming mouth and stabbed her. The old woman still wouldn't stop struggling, so he smashed her with the barrel of his gun and she finally went limp.

"Sonofabitch!" Sam said, blood running down his face from a deep cut over the bridge of his nose. "That old woman threw that lamp like a spear!" He looked at Alex. "How bad am I cut?"

Alex didn't hear the question because he was staring at the old woman, who was bleeding like a stuck hog. "She dead?"

"If she isn't, she will be soon enough," Tex said, stooping down to wipe his blade on the old woman's nightgown.

"She sure was a fighter for her age," Alex marveled. "And she's still fighting. I can see her chest moving up and down."

"Close her damned door!" Tex ordered.

They closed the door and all three of them watched the woman's death struggle. After a moment, Alex said, "Do you think she saw us clearly?"

"Hell yes she did," Sam growled as he pulled his own knife and cut the woman's throat from ear to ear. "But now that doesn't matter a gawdamn bit, does it, brother?"

"No," Alex said, swallowing hard and turning away as the woman's heels did a little death dance against the hardwood floor. "I suppose that it really doesn't."

Tex started nosing around, saying, "Maybe she has a bottle in here. I could use a drink right now."

"Me, too," Alex said.

Sam had found a towel and was trying to staunch the flow of blood down his face. He looked shaken and mad.

"Damn that old woman!" he swore, pulling the towel away to see if his deep laceration had stopped bleeding so profusely. It hadn't, so he cursed again and pressed the blood-soaked towel back against his head.

"Aha!" Tex said, finding a nearly full bottle of whiskey. "Here we go!"

Tex took a long and obviously satisfying pull on the bottle then handed it to Sam, who did the same. Alex surprised both men by swallowing a quarter of the bottle.

"Easy on that, kid! We still got the job to do and we better be sober."

"Don't call me 'kid' again," Alex warned. "I'm no kid, and someday I'll take my father's place."

Tex spat on the floor and shook his head. "You sure hold yourself in high regard."

"Maybe I do and maybe I don't, but—"

"Listen!" Tex hissed. "Someone is coming down the stairs. Tex ran to the door and opened it a crack, saying, "Get ready!"

A few seconds later he eased the door shut. "It's not the marshal and the girl."

Alex collapsed on an old horsehair sofa that had seen a lot better days. He felt like he was going to vomit, and he couldn't bear to look at the dead woman and the pool of blood caused by the slash his brother had administered to her throat. He hoped that she didn't have any kids that would come and discover her body the way it looked now. He couldn't even imagine how that would affect a person seeing her with that gaping horror and the white, gristly, and completely severed windpipe.

"Let's all just settle down and get ourselves ready for what we came to do," Tex said, eyes pinning each of the brothers. "So far we're doing just fine and this will hopefully be over with soon."

"Amen to that," Alex said, reaching for the whiskey.

"Enough!" Tex ordered, coming over to snatch the bottle away and then pouring it down the kitchen sink. "We got work yet to do, and by gawd we are going to do it right and get out of here without anyone seeing us or knowing what happened."

Alex looked to his brother and saw that Sam had a dazed expression on his big, brutish face as he stared at the dead woman near his feet. Despite his bluster and size, Sam Ramsey wasn't doing so well either, and for some reason that made Alex feel a whole lot better.

Chapter 16

Longarm and Rose slept late, and after coffee and some rolls that Rose had leftover from yesterday's run to the bakery, they both sat around for a little while, until Rose said, "Custis, I'm bored."

"I could suggest a few things we could do right here and now," he told her with an impish grin.

She put her hands on her hips. "Yeah, I'll just bet you could."

Longarm shrugged. "Well, you're right. We can't sit here stewing for days at a time. How about we take a walk over to my office?"

"I'd rather do a little shopping."

"We can do that, too," Longarm said agreeably. "We just have to stay in the crowds and not stand out to make ourselves easy targets."

A few minutes later they were ready to leave. Longarm checked the time and said, "It's too early yet for the shops to be open. Why don't we stop and have a leisurely breakfast?"

"I'd like that," Rose said, picking up the pistol that Longarm had given her and slipping it into the large pocket of her dress.

"That thing might fall out and raise some eyebrows," Longarm commented.

"It won't fall out," she promised. "Let's go."

Longarm unlocked the door and peered up and down the empty hallway. "All clear."

Rose kept her hand in her dress pocket, and although she looked calm and composed, her heart was beating fast because she knew that the Ramsey men would come all the way to Denver after her and the marshal.

Longarm stood at the top of the stairs and gazed down into the little foyer. There was no one in sight, although he was certain that Agnes had already been up and about. He had often wondered if his landlady ever slept, and if she opened her door to peek out at the backs of all the comers and goers among the tenants.

"Let's go," he said, hand near his belt buckle and not far from the butt of his Colt that rested on his left hip.

They started down the creaking stairs, and when they got to the foyer, Longarm reached for the door leading outside. Suddenly, he heard the faint and all too familiar squeak of Agnes's door hinges. Expecting the old woman to poke her nose out and offer a cryptic comment, Longarm turned and caught the sight of a boot and a big hand an instant before the door was thrown wide open.

Tex had his gun in his fist as Longarm threw himself at the door, catching a bullet across his forearm. The force of his collision slammed the door into the three waiting gunmen. Tex was knocked off balance, and Longarm was falling as Rose yanked her pistol out and fired through the half-opened door.

A man screamed, and Longarm rolled, grabbing his gun and shooting blindly upward. There was a second cry of pain, and then a tall, slender man with a fancy gun in his fist took an unsteady step forward, turning his aim at Rose. Longarm used his third bullet to fire upward into the man's crotch. Tex howled, and his gun flew from his hand as he grabbed his balls, mouth wide open. Longarm shot him again, and his bullet entered Tex's body just under his fancy gunbelt and exploded from the man's lower back after shattering his spine.

There were more shots, all fast and deafening. Rose hit the floor and rolled sideways. Longarm emptied his gun through the doorway, and a big man crashed over backward into Agnes's room.

The two larger men were on the floor, the biggest cursing and trying to lift his pistol and take aim. Longarm threw himself on the giant's body, tore the pistol from his hand, then used it to shoot him in the forehead.

"Shit!" the smallest of the three cried from farther back in the room, with blood pouring from wounds in his upper right leg as well as his shattered hip.

"Drop your gun!" Longarm ordered as he took a sure aim with the giant's pistol. "Drop it now!"

Alex Ramsey stared into the barrel of not only Longarm's weapon, but also the one that Rose Delamonte was holding. He knew in less than the blink of his eye that he was looking point-blank into the brink of a very, very black abyss that he desperately did not want to spiral down into.

He threw his gun away and sobbed, "Don't kill me!"

Longarm struggled to his feet, and Rose stepped into the room behind him. When they saw the old landlady with her throat cut from ear to ear, they momentarily froze in shock at the grisly sight.

"You sonofabitch!" Longarm growled, his gun slashing downward to savage Alex Ramsey's upturned face. "You murdered Agnes!"

"I didn't do it!" Alex blubbered. "I didn't kill her. Sam did!"

"Where are the others?" Longarm demanded.

"I don't know!"

"Liar! Where are the rest of your people?"

"There are no others!"

Longarm didn't believe it. "You're going to bleed to death right here in this room," he told the young man as he pulled out a handkerchief, spun it around, and prepared to use it as a gag. "And no one will hear your cries for help. There won't be any doctor and you'll be buried in the same dirty hole that these other two bastards will be buried in, without even the comfort of cheap pine coffins or wooden headstones. No one will ever know where you lie rotting in the grave, and no one in this city will ever care."

"Please," Alex begged, shaking his head back and forth and trying to twist away from the gag. His voice was growing faint. "I swear that I didn't want any part of this. They made me help them, but I refused to hurt the old lady."

"Oh?" Longarm asked with sarcasm. "But you were plenty ready to shoot Rose and me given half a chance."

Alex Ramsey's head drooped to his chest and tears flowed down his bloody cheeks as he wept. A big pool of blood was forming under him, indicating that a bullet had severed a big vein or artery in his leg.

"Where are they?" Longarm demanded, shaking the young man and trying to keep him from losing consciousness. "You've got more brothers. Did your father and sister come to Denver along with you three vipers?"

"No!"

Longarm grabbed the young man by his hair and started to wrap the gag around his mouth. From the amount of blood that he was losing, Longarm didn't give the kid more than five minutes.

"All right!" he whispered. "They're here, but I need a doctor."

"Where?" Longarm demanded. "What hotel and what rooms are they staying in?"

Alex Ramsey was as pale as a ghost, and his voice had dropped to a faint whisper. Longarm leaned closer, and Alex stared into his eyes, then his hand went into his vest as he tried to drag out a derringer.

Longarm batted the derringer away and stood up. "Unmarked common grave for all three of you in the pauper's part of the city cemetery."

"No," Alex breathed. "They are . . ."

Rose dropped to the young man's side and pleaded. "Alex, it's Rose. Tell us where they are!"

Alex blinked, and a small smile touched his lips as they moved.

"What?"

But the young man shivered and died.

"Did you hear what he said?" Longarm asked.

Rose covered her own face and in a low voice whispered, "Alex said . . . he said that he loved me."

Longarm collapsed on Agnes's couch and inspected the wound on his forearm. It was bleeding pretty good, but the bullet hadn't touched the bone and he knew that he would survive.

But look at the carnage now spread out tightly packed on the wooden floor right before his eyes. Agnes, a giant, what appeared to be a professional gunman, and the kid who had bled out pleading for more than a pauper's grave.

"Damn," Longarm said to himself. "What a hellish sight."

Rose came over to the couch and sat down beside him, then buried her face against his shoulder and wept.

"There are more," Longarm said quietly. "The kid said that there were more."

"And these dead will only make them more determined," Rose said. "Alex was his father's favorite even though he was the smallest. I always thought that he was better than any of them. Kinder. More sensitive."

"He would have killed us both, Rose."

"I know. But only because they gave him no choice."

"He could have run away from them. He had a choice, but he made the wrong one."

"He said he loved me," Rose said. "And for that I'll make sure he is buried with dignity and a headstone."

"Your money," Longarm told her. "Makes no difference to me. But I sure did want to find out where the rest of that bunch is holed up at."

She stared into his eyes. "Why don't we just leave town before they come for us?"

"Why would we do that?"

"I . . . I just don't want to have something like this happen again. I don't want to wait for them to try again."

"You want us to go to their ranch and wait for them?"

Rose nodded her head. "It's my ranch. And there is that gold and we could maybe hire some . . ."

Longarm nodded. "I'm sick of being bait. Let's go to New Mexico, Rose. That's the last thing that they'll expect."

"All right." She hugged him tightly. "Let's leave on the next train out of town."

"We're just putting off the inevitable showdown."

"I know. But . . . but I can't stand any more bloodshed right away."

"That's understandable."

Rose took a deep breath. She forced herself to look at Agnes. "Did you even like her?"

"Yeah, I did," Longarm confessed. "And somewhere inside her shriveled and meddling little heart, I think she basically liked me, too."

"Custis?"

"Can we just leave and have the authorities take care of all of this?"

"We can," he replied, helping Rose to her feet. "And by the way, you are sure one hell of a woman with a gun. I'd put you up against most anyone in my office."

"I told you that I could shoot straight."

"I know. But to be able to do that with gunfire all around is a rare show of courage, Rose. Rare indeed."

"Let's go," she said, taking his hand and pulling him up from the couch. "I don't want to ever step into this slaughterhouse of a room again."

"Me neither," Longarm admitted, helping her out of the door.

Chapter 17

Longarm somberly ushered Rose into his boss's office and closed the door. After Rose was seated, Longarm took a chair, crossed his long legs, and removed his hat to place it on the toe of his boot. He glanced sideways at the Santa Fe woman, who still appeared very pale and shaken.

Billy glanced from one to the other of them, not missing all the blood spatters on their clothes. He leaned forward with his arms resting on his desk. "I'm guessing that something very bad happened this morning."

"Very bad," Longarm answered. "Rose has identified two of the three men that laid an ambush for us in our apartment building. Two of them were Ramsey brothers."

"So," Billy said, "starting with Horace Ramsey and now two more of his brothers means that three of them are dead. Are there any other brothers?"

"One," Rose told them. "One brother and a sister."

"And the head of the clan, Mr. Amos Ramsey," Billy added.

"Yes," Rose agreed. "And that old man is going to be

out of his mind with grief and a thirst for bloody revenge."

"To hell with him!" Billy exploded. He gathered his composure and lowered his voice to say, "Custis, tell me exactly how they intended to catch you by surprise and in ambush."

"They murdered my landlady, whose name was Aggie. Then they hid out in her room near the exit door of the building. When Rose and I came downstairs to go for a walk and get some fresh air, all three men attacked."

"Did they come in from behind you?"

"Yes," Rose said. "They thought they had a perfect plan to catch us off guard."

"And what foiled that plan?"

Custis scowled. "A faint squeak of my landlady's door hinges. I've heard that sound a thousand times, and when I turned, I saw them starting to jump out into the foyer. Rose and I both were armed, and I think we got pretty lucky and managed to kill them before they killed us."

Billy looked deep into the New Mexico woman's eyes. "I'm sorry this happened. It must have been a terrible experience."

"It was," Rose admitted. "Especially the brutal way that Aggie was murdered using a knife across her throat."

"So there are four bodies currently lying in the landlady's apartment?"

"That's right," Longarm replied. "I didn't notify the authorities or the mortuary. I'm sure that some of the other tenants, having heard all the gunfire, have already sent for them."

"Yes," Billy agreed. "Custis, I'll need written statements from both of you, and I'll immediately send a couple of marshals over to your rooming house."

"Sounds like the thing to do, Boss."

"I'm sure it is. For right now, however, I think you and Mrs. Delamonte should find a new place to stay and hide."

"We've talked about that," Rose told him. "Marshal Long and I have decided to leave for Santa Fe on the next train."

Billy stared at them in disbelief. "But why in the world would you want to go to Santa Fe, where the Ramsey family is so powerful? My gawd, at least here in Denver we can offer you both some protection."

"We didn't have any protection about an hour ago," Longarm said tightly. "In fact, we had no protection whatsoever."

"I'm sorry. We should have come up with a better plan. Do you think that there are any more Ramsey people in town or were there only the three dead ones?"

Rose spoke up. "Alex Ramsey was the youngest and most favored son of Amos Ramsey. Alex didn't die instantly, and before he died he told us that there were more men from Santa Fe in this town."

"Did he say anything more?"

"Yes, but it had nothing to do with what is now important."

"Let me be the judge of that," Billy told her. "What else did young Ramsey say before he died?"

"He said," Rose whispered, "that he loved me."

This revelation caught Billy Vail completely off guard, and for a moment he did not quite know what to say. "Oh. Well . . . did the dying man say where the others were staying?"

"I think he tried to tell us," Rose replied. "But he died before that was possible."

"What I want to know," Longarm said, "is how those three knew *exactly* where we were in hiding."

"I'm sure that they just asked around," Billy offered.

"I suppose, but they found us so quickly that I'm wondering if there was any other way they could have learned about our location so fast."

Billy steepled his fingers and rested his chin upon them. "Custis, something is bothering you, so spit it out. What are you *really* thinking?"

"You told me that you had decided to send that fool Herb Pelkey to Santa Fe. Has he left yet?"

"I'm sure that he has."

"Well," Longarm decided, "I'll find him in Santa Fe, and I hope that he doesn't muck everything up there in advance."

"I know that you don't like Marshal Pelkey, and I can't say that I do either," Billy confessed. "But the man is not stupid and he's not greedy. Hopefully, Marshal Pelkey will have obtained some important information by the time you and Mrs. Delamonte arrive in Santa Fe."

"We'll see about that," Longarm replied, the tone of his voice leaving little doubt as to his skepticism. "But before we leave this town, we need to go around to the hotels and see if we can find Amos Ramsey or any of his men and get them behind bars."

"On what charges?" Billy asked. "They'd swear that they had nothing to do with the ambush this morning, and since they weren't even at the murder scene, I'm not sure we could arrest them."

"We could think of something!"

"Maybe, but probably not. We know they are all in this together, but proving it with three dead men in your landlady's room would be all but impossible."

Longarm hated to admit it, but Billy was right. "Listen," he said stubbornly. "At least we ought to try and find them before they find us. Rose can identify Amos Ramsey."

"Custis, do you really want to put Mrs. Delamonte's life in danger again?"

Rose stiffened. "With all due respect, Marshal Vail, I *insist* on going around to the city's hotels in the hope of spotting Amos, his daughter, and that sole remaining son."

"I see," Billy said.

Rose wasn't finished. "What worries me is that there may be more of the Ramsey men in Denver. That's why Custis and I believe we would be wise to leave town, which is the very last thing they'd expect."

"This whole thing is extremely dangerous, and I could order you not to leave Denver," Billy told them.

"But you won't," Custis shot back.

"No," Billy finally replied, "I won't, because it probably is smart to leave. Yet this whole thing about Mrs. Delamonte going from hotel to hotel searching for the Ramsey people really has me worried. What if they spot her before she sees them?"

"That's a chance I think we'll have to take," Longarm told his boss. "We'll give it only a few hours, and if we have no luck in finding Amos and his men, then we'll board this afternoon's train."

"All right," Billy agreed, "but I insist that a couple of our marshals accompany you around Denver."

"We can't appear to be a damned search party," Longarm growled.

"The deputies can stay at their distance and pretend to be ordinary citizens going or coming from work or just shopping."

"I want to pick them."

"Agreed," Billy said. "And now I need to send people

to your rooming house, where the bodies are waiting. Is there anything else we need to discuss before we end this meeting?"

"One thing," Rose told him, reaching into her purse and withdrawing money. "I want to pay for Alex Ramsey's funeral. I want the man to have a decent casket and a headstone with his name engraved on it. I refuse to allow Alex to be buried in a pauper's grave."

"May I ask why you care about the last remains of someone that tried to murder you and my marshal?" Billy asked.

Rose paused for a long moment, then said, "Alex was, I think, a decent person at heart. Had it not been for his father and evil brothers, I think he would have become a very fine man. He would probably have married well and raised good and law-abiding children. To my way of thinking, Alex was born into the wrong family and never really had a chance to become that fine man."

Billy nodded and took her money. "I'll see that Alex Ramsey is given a proper burial and that words are spoken over his grave."

"Thank you."

"Custis, who do you want shadowing you and Mrs. Delamonte around to the hotels this morning?"

Longarm told his boss the pair of men he most trusted.

"I'll get them right now, and we'll just hope this search turns up something fruitful," Billy said. "I'd like nothing better than to see the Ramsey bunch brought to justice, but we have to have some evidence that they were involved in this morning's attack."

"Let's find and arrest them if we can, shoot them down if we can't," Longarm snapped. "To hell with the evidence."

"Spoken true to form," Billy grumbled as he pushed

out of his office chair and got ready to get Longarm and Rose some help in this morning's dangerous search. "Oh, one question, Custis."

"Shoot."

"Were you at all close to your murdered landlady?"

Longarm shook his head. "No, I wasn't close to her, but I did care for Aggie, and I gave her a measure of my grudging respect. She didn't deserve to die like she did early this morning. I believe that she fought like hell before they killed her in that apartment."

"And what makes you think that?"

"The dead giant had a deep gash in his ugly face. Aggie must have been the cause of that wound, and also I just have the feeling that she was tough as boot leather and a real fighter . . . like Rose."

Billy turned to the woman. "Thank you for being so brave and helping my deputy, Mrs. Delamonte."

"You're welcome, and so is Custis. And don't forget that I was fighting for my own life at the same time I was fighting to help your marshal."

"Oh," Billy told her, "I would never forget something like that."

Chapter 18

"Custis, where do we start looking for them?" Rose asked as they stood on a busy street corner. "Compared to this city, Santa Fe is small."

Longarm had been giving that question his careful consideration as they stood before the Federal Building. "See that millinery just up the street a few doors?"

"Yes."

"Why don't you go inside and buy the biggest, floppiest hat they have in stock?" he suggested. "One that will hide your lovely face as we make the rounds this morning."

"I understand the reason for that, but I suppose just wearing your flat-brimmed hat would not be an acceptable idea."

"You've got that one right."

Rose offered him a forced smile. "I'll be right back, because buying a floppy lady's hat will not be fun and it will only take a few minutes."

"Don't get one so outlandish that it will attract everyone's attention," Longarm warned.

"I wouldn't dream of it," Rose told him as she hurried across the street and disappeared into the shop.

Longarm lit a cigar and glanced down the busy avenue until he spotted the two deputies that Billy had asked to help protect them. He motioned for both men to move apart and a little farther away. Longarm blew smoke, knowing that both lawmen were seasoned professionals. He watched the crowd moving along the street and noted that the day was already starting to warm up.

Rose appeared after about five minutes wearing a huge yellow hat with fake white daisies and matching ribbon. The hat's brim was so large that it drooped well over her forehead and ears, shadowing her face.

"What do you think?" she asked, not looking at all happy.

"It's perfect."

"I think it is gaudy and it was damned expensive."

"It will prove to be worth whatever you had to pay for the thing," Longarm assured her.

"I wouldn't be caught dead in Santa Fe wearing this monstrosity."

"There is a charity shop near the railroad depot where people donate items of clothing and whatever else would prove helpful to the less fortunate of our city. I'm positive that there are plenty of older women who would love to wear your new hat."

"Then that's where it will go before we board the train," Rose vowed. "Now, let's get busy checking out all the hotels."

"We'll start with the St. Michael's Hotel and work our way up one side of this street and then back down the other."

"Are all of Denver's hotels located on this street?"

"Only the biggest and the best," he told her. "Am I wrong to think that old Amos Ramsey would pick a fine hotel?"

"No, he'd do that."

"Then let's go," Longarm said, filled with a mix of anticipation as well as concern that one of the men that they were hunting would spot Rose first and kill her or him on sight.

The St. Michael's Hotel proved to be a bust, and so did the next four hotels where they entered and made their inquiries at the registration desk. At each hotel, Longarm would flash his federal marshal's badge and gain instant cooperation. And despite not being sure that he would get a positive response, he asked the hotel clerks if they had any new guests registered from New Mexico or whose names were Ramsey.

"I'm not sure this is the way to go about finding them," Rose told him. "Amos isn't dumb, and he'd never register under his own name or write down in the book where he and his men were from."

"I know that," Longarm said, "but there are dozens of new guests coming and going through these hotels every day, so do you have any better ideas?"

"I guess not."

"Then let's keep moving and asking."

At the sixth hotel, the impressive Vanderbilt, Longarm and Rose finally got lucky. A smallish, balding clerk at the registration desk whose name tag read "OSCAR" was more than helpful.

"Oh, they were staying here, all right," he told them. "Have they done anything wrong?"

Longarm ignored the question. "Have these people already checked out of this hotel?"

"They did, only a few hours earlier," Oscar answered. "They left about eight o'clock, after paying their bill, and I have to say that they were pretty upset looking."

"I'm sure that they were," Rose said.

"Did they murder anyone?" Oscar asked almost hopefully. "They were very hard-looking men, and they were heavily armed. Some of us employees were—"

"Oscar," Longarm said, cutting the man off in mid-sentence, "we're in a big hurry so would you just tell me what you can about them?"

Oscar's smile faded and he cleared his throat. "Uh, what exactly would you like to know?"

"For starters, describe the oldest of the men."

"The oldest was short and fat, but he looked strong and he wore a mustache, long and white. He had a pronounced limp."

"That's him!" Rose exclaimed. "That's Amos Ramsey."

Longarm continued to focus on Oscar. "Would you show me the registration book? I'd like to see how they registered into this hotel."

"Of course, Marshal. But I can tell you right now that they took three separate rooms and there wasn't an Amos Ramsey or any Ramsey registered at this hotel."

"That makes perfect sense given that they intended to murder us."

"Did you say, 'murder'?" Oscar blurted.

"Yes, that's what I said.

"May I ask . . ."

"All right, Oscar. But this is between us. Don't gossip what I'm about to tell you."

"Of course not!" Oscar whispered, lowering his voice and bending forward with anticipation.

Longarm frowned, knowing they wouldn't be out the

door before half the staff at this hotel would know why they were hunting Amos Ramsey and his men. "The ones we want are from out west."

"California?"

"Maybe," Longarm replied. "And they are very dangerous."

"I could have told you that much," Oscar told them. "How many men have they killed?"

"Quite a few. How many checked out of this hotel this morning in addition to the older man that you have just described?"

"There were two other men and I think there might have been a woman."

"Might have been?" Rose asked.

"Well," Oscar said quickly, "the woman was very beautiful, and she checked into our hotel a few hours before the others and left about a half hour after they left."

"Oscar, would you please describe her?" Rose asked.

"That's easy to do because she had the most beautiful long and blond hair and her eyes were deep blue. She had a high forehead, straight nose, and big . . . uh, well she wasn't skinny, I can tell you that for certain."

"That's got to be Etta Ramsey," Rose said. "And as good as she might have looked, she's as dangerous as a rattlesnake."

Oscar gulped. "She didn't look dangerous, but if you say so, ma'am."

"I say so," Rose told the small man.

"Well," Oscar said a bit ruefully, "there were plenty of men in this hotel who would have liked to find out if she was dangerous or not."

Longarm had to smile as he led Rose out of the hotel. "So they were here and they're gone."

"Maybe they went to the hotel depot to buy tickets for Santa Fe."

"Nope," Longarm said, "they wouldn't be that stupid."

"Then maybe they went to a stagecoach line," she offered.

"That's a real possibility," Longarm told her. "Or perhaps a livery where they could buy horses."

"Amos is too old to ride all the way back to New Mexico. And he had an accident on a horse in downtown Santa Fe that injured his back, so he can't ride much at all anymore."

"It's a shame the accident didn't kill the old man."

"It almost did. Amos was hurled to the ground by a bucking horse right in the middle of the town, near the plaza. And guess what happened next?"

"I'm not in the mood for guessing games, Rose."

"Well, Amos dragged his gun from his holster and shot the damned horse right in the middle of the street."

"Is that a fact?"

"It sure is, and I can tell you that it caused quite a stir."

"I imagine so."

"But you see, Amos is the most important banker in Santa Fe and he owns the local marshal. After a few days the fuss all settled down, but people are still upset about that dead horse and saying he could easily have killed an innocent bystander."

"If he'd have done that here in downtown Denver, he'd have gone to jail no matter how important he was or how much money he has. People around here wouldn't have put up with that kind of reckless behavior."

"Amos is old but he still has a terrible temper."

"I'll keep that in mind," Longarm assured her. "Now we need to start visiting the stables and stage companies."

"Then let's get to moving!"

Longarm and Rose hurried off down busy Colfax Avenue, completely unaware of the beautiful blonde who watched them intently for several minutes and then rushed away.

Etta Ramsey found her father in a café, eating a late breakfast. She hurried over to their table out of breath and whispered, "Father, they're combing the town looking for us, and Rose is leading the pack."

Amos's hand stopped with a forkful of pancake halfway to his mouth. He lowered the fork, looked around to make sure that they could not be overheard, and said, "Are you damn sure of that?"

"Of course I am! I just saw the big marshal that gunned down Horace. He was with Rose and they left the Vanderbilt Hotel less than ten minutes ago. We've got to get out of this town and we've got to do it fast."

"Damn!" Amos swore in anger, slamming his fork down into his half-eaten breakfast. "How the hell did they know we are in town?"

"Would it really be that hard to figure out?" Etta asked. "I mean, it's obvious that Sam, Alex, and Tex are dead, or we'd have seen them show up by now."

"Maybe they're locked up in jail or in some hospital," Amos offered, paying his bill and making a hasty exit outside.

"No," Etta insisted. "They're *dead*!"

Amos grabbed a porch post and heaved a heavy sigh. "Yeah, you're right. But I don't see how all three of them could have failed."

"Does it matter anymore?"

"No," Amos bitterly admitted, "it doesn't."

"Where are the others?"

"I sent them out of town when we checked out of that hotel," Amos answered. "I had a feeling that things were going against us and it seemed the smart thing to do."

"It *was* the smart thing to do," Etta agreed. "And now we've got to find a way out of this town before we're caught and arrested."

"On what charges?" Amos demanded. "They can't prove a damn thing."

"We're not in Santa Fe," Etta said tersely. "Do you really want to go before a judge and explain why two of your sons died this morning trying to kill a woman and a federal marshal?"

"No."

"Then let's just get out of here and get back to Santa Fe!"

"And leave that marshal and Rose Delamonte to gloat in triumph?"

"Father, this is no time to get your back up and be proud," Etta said harshly. "We failed here. Don't you understand that yet?"

"I understand that three of my sons . . . your brothers . . . have died in this gawdamn town, and I want revenge!"

Etta grabbed her father and pulled him close. "Listen to me! We are up against it here in Colorado. We came to get even, and all we did was get more family killed. We have to cut our losses in Denver and get back where we belong and where we hold the advantage."

"But what . . ."

"They'll come to New Mexico for us," Etta promised. "That big marshal was hanging all over Rose. And she'll have told him about what we did to her husband and how we finagled a way to steal her ranch. And she will also have told him that there is money to be made. A lot more money than a United States marshal could ever make on his job. So I promise you, Father, they will come to Santa Fe, and when they do, we will kill them."

"I want to torture them first. The marshal who killed my boys and then that Delamonte woman. I want to hear her scream and see her blood flow, gawdammit!"

"You will," Etta said passionately. "You will. But on our ground. In our part of the country."

Amos finally nodded and allowed himself to be led away. Etta was trying to move fast. If they could just get out of Denver, she knew that they would have their day. They would have their just revenge and take their blood. She wasn't sure if she could stand the sight of Rose Delamonte being raped, cut, and tortured, but she would not deny her father his due and his pleasure.

"Hurry!" she pleaded, practically pulling the limping old man down the boardwalk as fast as he could move. "Hurry!"

Chapter 19

Longarm and Rose had to move fast in order to visit all the livery stables and the two biggest stagecoach lines in Denver. Afterward, they raced back to their rooming house, not wanting to look inside Aggie's place, where there were still people working to clean up the scene of four bloody deaths.

"Hey!" one local officer shouted as Longarm started up the stairs. "Our sheriff wants to see you down at his office right away. There are reports to fill out, and he's not happy about the fact that you two haven't visited him yet."

"We're heading there as soon as we grab a few things and leave the building," Longarm promised the local lawman.

"Which one of these dead bastards slit the old woman's throat?"

"I've no idea," Longarm yelled over his shoulder as he took the stairs two at a time.

"And how did you kill all three of them!" the man shouted up the stairway.

"I got lucky and had help!"

Longarm and Rose both hurried into their rooms to grab what they would need for the extended time they would be gone. The yellow cat was meowing and carrying on, so Rose banged on her neighbor's door and gave the man fifty dollars to take care of Charlie for as long as necessary.

Longarm had forgotten the man's name, but he was a retired fellow in poor health. He heard him say to Rose, "Mrs. Delamonte, fifty dollars will feed Charlie for a year or better."

"Just feed him well," Rose said. "And make sure that he stays inside when the weather is miserable."

"I'll do that," the old man vowed. "I always liked Charlie."

Rose went back into her room and stuffed clothes and belongings into a pair of suitcases. She met Longarm out in the hallway, and he had a heavy canvas duffel bag filled with his own necessities, as well as a Winchester rifle and plenty of ammunition.

"You ready?" he asked, even as they heard the first blast of the train telling everyone in town that it was about to leave the Denver station.

"I'm ready," Rose answered.

"Then let's get out of here."

"What about the officer downstairs and that report we were supposed to write?"

"Maybe a telegram from Santa Fe will do."

"It would have to be a long one."

Longarm shrugged. "The government can afford it."

"Hey!" the lawman downstairs shouted as they swept through the foyer and out onto the street. "What . . ."

Neither Longarm nor Rose took the time to respond, but instead they moved swiftly down the street toward the train station.

"We can buy our tickets from the conductor after we're under way," Longarm told her as they pushed through the foot traffic. "I sure hope they have a sleeping compartment available."

"*Two* of them," Rose added.

"Yeah, that's what I meant," Longarm said, out of breath as he helped Rose and her baggage on board, just as the train lurched forward and began to roll. "Rose, take the first seat you can find and I'll find the conductor and get us settled in."

"All right," she said, chest heaving as she fought for the thin air.

Longarm crammed his big canvas duffel into an empty space and sought out the conductor. He had traveled this line so often that he knew them all, and he was pleased when he found one of his favorites, Conductor Augustus "Gus" Bonner.

"We just made it on board," Longarm explained.

"Good to have you with us again," Gus replied, shaking Longarm's hand. "We always feel a little safer when we have a famous lawman on board."

Longarm blushed. "Not too many train robberies to worry about lately, Gus."

"Yeah, but you never know when it will happen next."

"Are all the private sleeping compartments taken on this run?"

"Got a couple left." Gus raised a bushy eyelid. "I saw you and a mighty pretty woman running for the train. What are you thinking, Marshal Long?"

"I'm thinking that you only have one sleeping compartment available," Longarm told him with a wink of his eye. "A nice, private one."

Gus Bonner shook his head. "You're a man who never seems to want to sleep."

"I'll sleep in my grave," Longarm told him as he grabbed his canvas duffel bag. "Lead the way, Gus."

Not all sleeping compartments were the same size on this train. There were, Longarm knew, several doubles that had been created for dignitaries and very wealthy couples. Most often, they were empty because of their high cost, and Gus and the other conductors who liked Longarm so much made sure that he got a surprisingly good rate.

"Here you go," Gus said, opening the door and allowing Longarm to enter first. "I think you've used this one a time or two, with a woman or two."

"We keep our secrets, Gus. Remember that."

"I wish I had the kind of secrets you have to keep," the conductor said with an amused smile. "Will you be wanting wine or whiskey?"

"Some of both."

"I'll see that everything is just right for you and the lady, Marshal."

"You always do," Longarm said, slipping the man a generous tip.

Ten minutes later Longarm found Rose Delamonte sitting next to the window and gazing out at the outskirts of southern Denver. "It's a thriving city," she said as Longarm took a seat next to her. "Did you make our sleeping arrangements?"

Longarm shrugged and sighed. "I'm afraid that they only had *one* available private sleeper," he said as if this were about the worst news imaginable. "So of course I took it."

She smiled and patted his knee. "I'm glad that you did. How much do I owe the conductor?"

"Oh, don't worry about that now. I'm going to take care of it."

"Nonsense!" Rose reached into her purse. "I insist on paying for *my* accommodations."

"Actually," Longarm said, "the compartment is mine, arranged for and paid for by my federal office."

"What?"

"Yep."

"Then you'll just have to rent it to me."

"I can't do that, Rose. My back acts up if I sit in these seats too long. But the compartment is one of the largest on this train and there is plenty of room for us both."

She took her hand off his knee. "Ha! I see your clever and devious game."

Longarm tried on his most innocent expression. "Rose, it's a long, long way to Santa Fe, and we don't know who is on this train."

"Dammit, back in town you convinced me that Amos Ramsey would never be stupid enough to take this train back to New Mexico."

"I don't think he would, but it's possible. This train has more than six passenger cars."

"Then we'd better get busy and march through them to make sure that neither Amos nor Etta is on board."

"Oh, sure, we'll do that all right. But what if Amos has a hired gun or two on board? A couple of ringers that you would have no way of recognizing. After all, you told me that you didn't recognize that man with the fancy gun we shot in Aggie's apartment this morning."

Rose shook her head. "You're right, there could be another hired gunman on board that I have never seen before."

"Well there you have it then," Longarm said, trying to hide his satisfaction at having won the argument. "My thought is just to stay in our sleeping compartment and out of harm's way as much as possible."

Rose's brow furrowed with concentration, and she finally said, "All right, but you have to be on your very best behavior. I'm a *married* woman, Custis, and I'm not at all certain that you put any stock in that fact."

Longarm wanted to tell Rose that she *had been* a married woman, but he figured that would not be in his best interests, so he nodded and came back to his feet. "Give me those bags and let's get settled in together."

Rose stood and yawned. "I didn't sleep at all well last night, and after the nightmare of this morning, I'm exhausted."

"I could use some sleep, too, before we get down to Pueblo, where we'll have a stopover and dinner."

"I'm not a bit sure about this," Rose said as she followed Longarm up the aisle toward their sleeping compartment. "Not sure at all."

"I am," Longarm whispered happily to himself.

Chapter 20

Longarm and Rose Delamonte took a nap and didn't wake up until they rolled into the sleepy little town of Colorado Springs. Longarm stuck his head out of their compartment and saw one of the attendants moving down the aisle.

"Pssst!"

"Yes, sir?"

"Will you tell Gus, I mean Conductor Bonner, that I'd like to see him for a moment?"

"Of course. He's in the next car, and I'll ask him to come by as soon as he can."

"Thanks."

When Gus arrived a short time later, Longarm invited him into their sleeping compartment. "Conductor Bonner, this is Rose Delamonte."

Gus bowed slightly and removed his cap. "My pleasure."

"We'd like some whiskey and some champagne," Longarm told the man.

"'Champagne'?" Rose asked. "Why?"

"Because we're lucky to be alive given what happened

back at the apartment. And because I believe that sometimes, if you drink to a celebration before it happens . . . it
does happen."

Rose looked very skeptical. "That's a first for me, but I
do love champagne."

"And ours is an excellent French vintage," the conductor assured them. "Will you want two bottles on ice?"

"One is probably enough along with the whiskey, which
I assume is Hamilton's Special Reserve?"

"Yes, it is," Gus said proudly. "The best that money can
buy to my way of thinking."

"When will dinner be served?"

"Not until we get to Pueblo, ma'am. That's still a good
two hours from now. However, I can have some hors
d'oeuvres brought along with the liquid refreshments."

"I'd like that," Rose said. "And since the government is
paying for this lovely sleeping compartment, please put
this on my bill, Conductor Bonner."

Gus glanced at Longarm, who nodded. "Whatever the
lady wishes."

"Very good," Gus said happily a moment before he
ducked outside.

Five minutes later they were sipping champagne and
enjoying some wonderful cheeses, smoked salmon, and
crackers. Rose licked her lips and smiled. "You're a devious devil, Custis, but you seem to know how to get the
best of things on this train."

"I'm a regular passenger and I tip well," Longarm said.
"And also the staff likes to hear about some of my work,
so I indulge them . . . liberally embellishing my accom-
plishments, of course."

"Of course. I've never tasted better champagne," she

admitted, "but the truth is I've rarely had the opportunity to enjoy it."

"Then I'm glad we could do this, and we will order some every evening until we reach Santa Fe."

"I still can't believe what happened this morning," Rose said after they had nearly finished the bottle. "It was so horrible."

"It was," Longarm agreed. "But perhaps it would help if I told you that Aggie had a very bad stomach cancer."

"She did?"

Longarm nodded. "Of course, she never told anyone, but I have my sources and I knew the old gal had very little time left. I ran into her doctor and he said she was suffering and he'd been giving her increasingly large prescriptions for laudanum."

Tears filled Rose's eyes. "I wish I'd have known Aggie better."

"No, you don't," Longarm said. "She was a very disagreeable and lonely woman. Even so, I had a grudging admiration for the way she tried to hide her situation and pain."

"I should have offered to pay for her burial in the same way I did for Alex Ramsey."

"The people in the house will take up a collection. The old fella that you gave money to on behalf of the cat will kick in generously. He's got a heart condition and probably won't make it another year."

"How very sad!"

"Yes, but I will take Charlie in when I return to Denver, and that cat will probably outlive everyone in the building. Charlie is a survivor."

"So are you," Rose said. "I can't even imagine how

many men you've had to kill and how many have tried and failed to put you in the ground."

"Quite a few." Longarm stared out the window at the sunset, not even wanting to remember all the killing both during the War Between the States and what he'd been a part of as a deputy United States marshal. There were so many that the really scary part was he couldn't even remember all their faces anymore.

Rose moved over close to him and took his hand in her own. "You're thinking about all the death you've seen in your life."

"Yes, I am, and I shouldn't be."

"I've had a lot of death to try to live with in the last year."

"I know."

She laid her head against his chest. "I told you that I loved my late husband."

"Yeah, you told me that."

"But he's gone and I've got to try to put that all in the past."

"Even as we are going back to Santa Fe?"

She nodded. "I need to right the wrongs. That way I'll finally put it all to rest."

"Rose, when we get your ranch back and dig up that gold, I don't want any of it for myself. Maybe just a little to put away for a good burial if I am killed at my work."

"You'll have to take half of the gold," she told him. "That was our deal and I won't stand for you changing what we agreed upon."

Seeing that she wasn't going to budge right now on this issue, Longarm said, "You know what I'd really like?"

She lifted her head. "No, tell me."

"I'd like to make love to you."

Rose pulled back and stared into his eyes. "I'm . . . I'm afraid that I wouldn't pleasure you very much, Custis. I'm afraid that I might cry my husband's name and ruin everything."

"Late husband, Rose. I'm not trying to erase his memory or diminish it in any way. I'm trying to show you that there is hope for you tomorrow. Hope for justice and hope for a new love."

She sighed. "And maybe you will be that new love."

"Maybe, but maybe not. I don't know what tomorrow will bring. I only know that I want to make love to you right now."

She gulped and drained her glass of champagne. "Can we open that bottle of whiskey that is so heralded by your friend the conductor?"

"Are you trying to work up enough courage to make love to me?" Longarm asked her outright. "Because, if that is what you have to do, then I'll pass on the lovemaking and stick to the whiskey."

"Just open the bottle and don't talk for a few moments," she asked. "Please?"

"All right."

Longarm opened the bottle and poured them both generous amounts of the whiskey. He sniffed his glass and smiled, then offered Rose her glass, and they both raised them in a toast.

"To tomorrow," she said gazing into his eyes.

"To tomorrow and to love."

They drank, and then Rose set her glass down and began to undress. She was gorgeous to behold, and Longarm sipped his whiskey as he watched the lady take one garment off after the other, until she was as naked as a baby.

"My gawd, Rose!" he said in voice hoarse with desire. "You're a beautiful woman."

"Your turn," she whispered.

Longarm got out of his clothes about as fast as ever he'd undressed, and when he stood before her, his erection was huge and stiff. "Rose," he said, looking down at himself, "I'm not going to be able to hold off very long the first time we do this."

"I don't care. Right now I need to be loved. You can take me on the bed or standing here like we are . . . I don't care. Just do it to me, Custis, and don't hold back."

Longarm moved forward like a bull and impaled her against the wall. She moaned and he lifted her up, while she wrapped her legs around his hips. The rocking of the train was all the motion they needed as Longarm and Rose kissed and held each other tightly.

"Deeper," she whispered into his ear. "Harder!"

Longarm was far too much a man and a gentleman to deny a lady, and Rose Delamonte was a lady. So he obliged her, and their locked embrace and intense union lasted at least five rocking railroad miles.

Longarm took Rose again after dinner and later in the night when the train was taking on fuel and water. He had her for breakfast and then the next day just before lunch.

"I'm walking bowlegged," she said as they fell into a sleep and their train struggled up over Raton Pass. "You're going to have to give it a rest or I'll be the talk of Santa Fe when I waddle off the train."

"All right," he said. "But I have no idea what is waiting for us when we get to Santa Fe, so I think we'd better not miss any opportunities."

"We haven't been," Rose said. "And if I'm with your

child, you'd better marry me when we've taken care of the last Ramsey men and gotten my ranch back."

"I'll marry you if that's the way it works out."

"In that case," Rose said, cocking a finger for him to come to her again, "let's do it right on top of the pass."

Longarm laughed and mounted her yet again.

Chapter 21

Longarm and Rose stepped off the train in Santa Fe and wasted no time heading for the local sheriff's office. When they stepped inside, Sheriff Lucas Mandrake Greer had just finished brewing a fresh pot of coffee, which he was about to enjoy while perusing the daily news. But at the sight of Longarm and Rose Delamonte, he froze for a moment and simply stared at his unwelcome guests.

"Sheriff Greer," Rose said without bothering to shake the man's hand or offer him the faintest of a smile, "this is Deputy United States Marshal Custis Long and we've just gotten off the train from Denver."

Greer set his coffeepot down and cleared his throat. "My, my, the second federal marshal to come here in the last week. Things must be a little slow back in Denver."

"Not at all," Longarm said, coming forward and taking measure of the man. "Quite the opposite, actually. The very first thing I need to know is the whereabouts of Marshal Herb Pelkey."

"Damned if I know," Greer said, throwing up his hands.

"He got off the train just like you did and also came by this office to make his formal introduction. We talked and—"

"What did Marshal Pelkey want to talk to you about?" Longarm interrupted.

Sheriff Greer turned his back on them and poured a cup of coffee. "Would you both like a cup? I make a good, strong coffee."

"I'll have one," Longarm said.

"No, thank you," Rose told the sheriff. "As I'm sure you have guessed, we're not here to exchange pleasantries. We're here for *justice*."

Sheriff Greer slowly poured Longarm's cup of coffee while keeping his back to his guests, not wanting them to see how much he was struggling to pretend that everything was fine under his watch in Santa Fe.

"There you are, Marshal Long. Why don't you and Mrs. Delamonte have a seat and we can talk things out. My deputies are off duty right now, and we won't be interrupted unless there is some emergency that I'm called out to suddenly take care of."

Longarm took a seat at an empty office desk. "I think you know why we're here, and I'm still waiting to know more about Marshal Pelkey. What has he been doing and where can I find him?"

"I'm afraid," Greer said, "that I can't be of much help."

"Can't, or don't want to be of much help?"

Greer stiffened, then sipped his coffee for a moment before he spoke. "Marshal Pelkey, as I just told you, came in two days ago and he was exhausted. He sat right where you're sitting now, Marshal Long. And, as with you, I showed him my professional courtesy and hospitality by pouring him a cup of coffee. Several cups, actually."

"And what did the marshal tell you?" Longarm asked.

"He said that he had come to investigate the death of Mr. and Mrs. Delamonte, who died in a carriage accident and whose deaths were preceded by the death of their son."

"My husband, and he was *murdered*!" Rose swore.

To Longarm's surprise, Greer nodded with agreement. "There is no doubt that your husband was ambushed and shot to death. Where I think we differ in our opinions concerns *who* committed the murder and why."

"Who else had a motive other than Amos Ramsey!" Rose shot back. "Who else stood to gain so much by their deaths? You aren't a complete idiot, Lucas. How can you just sit and do nothing about this?"

Sheriff Greer's face turned red with anger or embarrassment. He swallowed another gulp of coffee and said, "Rose, I know that you are certain Amos Ramsey was behind the murder off all three of your relatives. But I also know that when the accident and the ambush occurred, Amos and his sons were right here in town staying at the Hacienda Hotel. I checked their registration book, and I interviewed witnesses who swore that the Ramsey men were present when all three deaths occurred."

"Of course they were here! They *hired* someone to do the killings."

"That, I'm sorry to say, is just your opinion. You can't take people to trial based solely on an opinion."

Rose turned pale with anger. "It's the opinion of almost everyone not employed by Amos Ramsey or under his control."

"That may be true but . . ."

Rose wasn't finished. "And I'll tell you something else, Lucas. You are up for reelection this fall, and people are going to toss you out of this office because of these unsolved murders. My husband and his parents were very well respected and liked in Santa Fe, and all the money that Amos Ramsey will throw into getting you reelected won't count for anything when people step up to the ballot box."

"Unfortunately, you are probably right about that," Greer said quietly. "I'm not deaf or dumb, and I hear all the local talk. My wife is worried sick that I won't have a job after October and we'll have to leave Santa Fe. My daughter is also worried half to death about leaving and losing all her friends. This is the only town she has ever known, and if I am replaced, I'm sure the new town sheriff won't want to carry around my dirty baggage. He'll have me clean out my desk and be gone within an hour of his election victory."

Longarm said, "Then perhaps you should step over to the right side of things and help us find not only Marshal Pelkey, but also who really shot and killed the Delamonte couple and Rose's husband."

"I'd like to do that, I really would," Sheriff Greer said with sincerity. "But I've already told you that Marshal Pelkey came to talk to me about the Delamonte deaths, then checked into the Hacienda Hotel and was never seen again."

"Did you ask around about his whereabouts?" Longarm challenged. "If Pelkey is still in town, he must be held hostage or he's dead and his body hidden. If he left town, he would have had to rent a horse or buggy."

"He didn't leave town in a rented buggy or on a rented horse," Greer assured them. "I've interviewed anyone who could have rented your federal marshal a horse or buggy, and they swear that they did not."

Longarm frowned.

"Look," Greer said, shoulders slumping, "if you don't

believe me, then ask the same people that I asked and I swear that you'll get the same answers. No one saw Marshal Pelkey after he had dinner that night."

"Where did he eat?"

"Right at the Hacienda Hotel. They have a small restaurant that serves pretty good food. Marshal Pelkey ate a rare steak that night by himself and drank a bottle of their best red wine. He appeared to be very tired according to both the chef and the waiter who served him. They said the Denver federal law officer told them that he was in Santa Fe investigating multiple murders."

"Pelkey told them that?" Longarm asked, finding it hard to believe that the man could be so stupid as to tip his hand and state his official business among the locals.

"Yes, he did, and the same waiter and chef will be working this evening. Ask them for yourself if you don't believe me."

"Oh," Longarm promised, "I fully intend to do so."

"And you'll receive the exact same answer that I did. They both swore that Pelkey was either a little drunk or he was very, very tired, because as he was leaving he lurched into a table and overturned it."

"Were there any other witnesses in the dining room at the time this happened?" Longarm asked.

"Yes, and I'll give you their names and tell you where they can be found."

"I'd appreciate that. What happened after Pelkey knocked over a dining room table?"

"He got angry at the waiter and pretended it wasn't his fault. Marshal Pelkey said the tables were set too close together for a man to move easily toward the doorway. He cursed the waiter, retrieved the tip he'd left on his table, and stomped out of the restaurant. The waiter then saw Pelkey stagger across the lobby and go upstairs to his hotel room."

"Never to be seen again."

"That's right," Greer said. "Never to be seen again."

Longarm scratched his cheek as his mind raced checking through all the possibilities. "Did you get the hotel to open up Pelkey's room in case he might have died of heart failure or some other natural cause?"

"Of course."

"And?"

"There was *nothing*," Greer told them. "Not the marshal and not any of his belongings, either."

"Had the bed even been slept in?"

"The bedspread was rumpled, but the bed didn't appear to have been slept in yet."

"Was there a fire escape or some exit that the officer could have used to sneak out or be taken out of the hotel without being seen?"

"There is a fire escape ladder," Greer told them. "I checked that, and I couldn't tell if it had been used recently."

Longarm scowled and looked to Rose for any additional questions she might have. "Lucas," Rose asked, "were there any fresh wagon wheel tracks under the fire escape or even sets of footprints?"

"I don't know," he admitted, sipping his coffee and trying to hide his embarrassment. "I . . . I didn't think to look."

"What room number did Pelkey have?"

"Room seven."

"Facing the front of the street or a back alley?" Rose asked.

"Back alley."

Longarm and Rose exchanged glances and knew they

were both having the same thought, and that was that Pelkey had been overwhelmed either by force or by drugs, or both, and hoisted or pushed through the window.

"We'll go look at the back alley for signs of foul play," Longarm told the man, setting his half-full cup of coffee on the desk and rising to leave.

"I will go with you," Sheriff Greer said, grabbing his hat. "It'll save time, and I want to be there as a witness to whatever is found. Don't forget, this is *my* town and it's still *my* investigation."

"I had the feeling that the investigation you were conducting was over," Longarm told the man.

"Not by a damned sight!"

"That's good to hear," Longarm told the local lawman as they hurried outside and down the street toward the Hacienda Hotel.

They stood in a trash-filled alley lined with one- and two-holed shitters to accommodate the needs of the various businesses flanking the big hotel. The trash and litter had spawned hordes of black flies and the stench was hard to take. Even so, there was a narrow alley where goods and supplies could be hauled by the wagonload to the rear doors of businesses.

Sheriff Greer craned his head back and pointed. "That would be Room seven," he said, pointing. "No doubt about it."

Longarm and Rose stared up at the hotel window. It was plenty large enough to climb through and there was a fire escape ladder close to the window.

"Look!" Rose said, pointing to the many hoofprints close by. "They're not very old. Boot prints, too."

Longarm and Greer examined them. Greer said, "It's

hard to say, but it looks like there were at least three horses and a couple of men."

"And they are only a day or two old," Longarm added.

"But no wagon tracks."

"Nope."

All three of them cogitated on this evidence, and then Longarm knelt and stirred the dirt with his forefinger. He came up with some irregularly shaped black clots. "This is dried blood."

"Are you certain?" Greer asked.

"I'd bet on it."

"Then," Greer said, "your federal marshal must have been forcibly removed from his hotel room upstairs, but . . ."

Longarm was ahead of the man. "It doesn't matter whether or not Marshal Pelkey was alive or dead when he was dropped or thrown down here into the alley."

"What do you mean by that?" Rose asked.

"You know what I mean," Longarm told her. "There's little doubt that the man is dead."

"But what about the body?" the sheriff asked.

"They could have draped it over the back of a horse," Longarm told them. "But what would have been the point? If they'd done that, they'd have risked someone seeing them, and that's not a sight easily forgotten. My guess is that Marshal Herb Pelkey's body is still in this alley covered by rubbish or . . ."

"Or what?" both Greer and Rose whispered.

"Shoved into one of these shitters," Longarm said, mouth twisting downward at the corners.

"Oh, my gawd!" Rose breathed heavily, looking shaken to the core. "You can't be serious!"

"I wish I wasn't being serious, but I'd bet a bunch that

he's within fifty feet of where we're standing." Longarm expelled a deep breath. "Sheriff Greer, this is still your town. If you want to keep it, then you'll find the body and have it taken to your favorite mortuary and examined. I'm certain that you'll find clear evidence that Pelkey was either stabbed, had his head caved in, or was strangled to death."

"Holy shit," Sheriff Greer whispered. "A federal marshal murdered less than a hundred yards from my office. I . . . I don't know what to say."

"Best not say anything until you or your deputies find the body and have it examined."

"If he's in one of these shitters . . ." Greer couldn't even finish his unspeakable thought.

Longarm looked deep into the man's stricken eyes. "It's *your* job to see this investigation through and uphold the law, Sheriff Greer. But if you think that this is as bad as it will get here in Santa Fe, you'd better think again."

To his credit, Lucas Greer nodded, raised his chin, and said, "I admit that I am influenced by Amos Ramsey, but I've never bent the law or lied to a judge or jury in Ramsey's behalf."

"No," Longarm said, "I doubt that you have. But what I think is that you've allowed yourself to become lazy and lax in your duties. You took Ramsey's campaign contributions and let things slide. Now it's time to either fish or cut bait."

"I'll do my duty, and wherever the evidence leads, I'll follow it no matter what personal consequences I'll face."

"Spoken like a true officer of the law," Longarm said. "We'll check into a hotel and see you later."

"Where will you be staying?" Greer asked. "Finding Marshal Pelkey's body might take a while."

"I hope he's buried under these piles of trash instead of shoved down in a shitter," Longarm said. "Because hauling his worthless dead ass out of there wouldn't be a job that I'd wish on my worst enemy."

Sheriff Greer blinked. "You said he was *worthless*."

"That's right."

"So he wasn't . . . wasn't a friend?"

"If he was," Longarm admitted, "I wouldn't be leaving this to you right now. I'd be staying here and helping find the fool."

Greer nodded as if he fully understood, and then he headed off quickly to find his deputies as well as anyone else that he could arm-twist into this sickening search for a federal lawman's body.

Chapter 22

Longarm and Rose met Sheriff Greer that evening at the Hacienda Hotel, where they ate dinner and then interviewed the waiter, chef, and two others who had witnessed Marshal Herb Pelkey's behavior the night he went missing.

Now it was growing late and the three of them sat at the table, the only ones remaining. Suddenly, one of Lucas Greer's deputies burst into the nearly empty dining room and rushed up to their table.

"Sheriff, you'd better come with us right now," he said breathlessly. "We found that missing federal marshal from Denver."

"Where?" Greer asked tersely.

"Under a big double-seater about twenty yards down the alley." The deputy, a young man with sandy-colored hair, looked badly shaken. "He was down into it, Sheriff. And some people during the last day or so must not have seen him under them because they . . ."

"Never mind!" Greer snapped. "Did you haul him out?"

"Yes, sir. We paid two drunks five dollars to do it and they earned every penny. They both got sick as hell and puked all over the place."

Greer looked across the table at Longarm. "So we found your missing marshal. How do you want us to handle this?"

"After the mortuary examination, have Marshal Pelkey cleaned up, given fresh clothes, and then bury him in your cemetery. I don't have any of the particulars of his life, so our office will send you information later for the headstone."

"Did the man have a wife and kids?"

"Not to my knowledge," Longarm said. "Pelkey had no one except a few politically important relatives in Washington, D.C., as far as I know. Marshal Pelkey should *never* have been allowed to wear an officer's badge."

"We'll get him buried in the Oak Crest Cemetery."

Longarm turned his attention to the young deputy. He was afraid to look sideways at Rose, who he knew would be extremely upset. "Deputy," Longarm asked, "I'm sure that it was a hideous sight, one that is not going to be easily forgotten."

"No, sir! None of us who saw what was dragged out of that shitter is likely ever to forget the sight or smell."

"But what I want to know," Longarm continued, "is did you see any other sign of foul play?"

"Sure did! The whole right side of the marshal's head had been beaten into pulp. It was clear to see right away."

Longarm looked at Sheriff Lucas Greer. "So you heard it from your own deputy's mouth. A federal officer has been murdered at the Hacienda Hotel. In *your* town."

"I heard it."

"Sheriff, you have a choice to make right now. You can

either help us . . . or oppose us, but you can't straddle the fence."

Greer's cheek muscles corded. "I don't understand what you are saying."

"Hell yes you do. Amos Ramsey is not in Santa Fe, but he and whatever people he has left are coming, and you can well imagine that when he arrives there is going to be a showdown. When that happens, you're either with the man who is standing behind all these murderers, or you and your deputies are standing side by side with me and Rose Delamonte. It has to be one way or the other."

After a long pause, Greer said, "I know that."

"Well, then?"

Sheriff Greer looked at his deputy. "Andy, you're a good man and you've started a new family. You just heard what the federal marshal said . . . so how do you feel about this?"

Andy was tall and skinny, but a handsome enough young man. He wrung his hands for a minute before speaking. "I've always been sure that the Delamontes were murdered by Mr. Ramsey and that their little ranch and all their stock were taken from them unlawfully. I think it's time we stand up for justice."

"But you know we don't have any proof against Amos or any of his people, and the judge came down on Mr. Ramsey's side on every issue brought before him."

"That's because the judge is paid under the table by Mr. Ramsey. Everyone knows Judge Harper is as crooked as a dog's hind leg. What I want to know, Sheriff, is have *you* also been taking Ramsey money all these years?"

Sheriff Greer came out of his chair, and his cheeks were crimson with anger. He was about the same height as his deputy, but fifty pounds heavier and right at the moment a whole lot madder. "Andy, I'm going to forget that you ever asked me that question."

"Yes sir."

Greer turned to Longarm. "I guess it's time I took a stand. I'll back you, Marshal Long. I'll back you and Rose, and we'll do whatever it takes to bring justice to your family, ma'am."

"I'm glad to hear that," Longarm said with relief.

"So am I," Rose told him.

"Me, too," Andy said with a broad grin. "So what happens now?"

Longarm studied everyone. "We ride out to the Delamonte ranch late tonight and overtake however many men are there and are willing to fight for Amos Ramsey."

"There won't be many," Rose said. "Last I heard there was just a cook, a wrangler, and a couple of cowboys that probably aren't interested in dying for the old man or his bunch."

"I hope that you're right," Longarm said. "How far is it to the ranch?"

"Eight miles to the north."

Longarm extracted his pocket watch then looked at the sheriff and his deputy. "It's a little past ten o'clock. Sheriff, can you and your deputies be ready to ride by midnight and have a couple of horses for Rose and myself?"

"That's easily done, but I'll leave one deputy here just in case there is trouble in town. My other deputy is sick in bed."

"I want to ride with you," Andy said, his young face tight with excitement. "I know those cowboys out at that ranch. We grew up together, and if I'm with you, then I'm sure there won't be any shooting."

"That sounds good," Longarm told the deputy. "We'll

see you and the sheriff in front of this hotel in about two hours."

When Sheriff Greer and his deputy had hurried off, Longarm and Rose walked over to the room they had gotten earlier at the Adobe Hotel. They entered the room and collapsed on the bed side by side.

"Well, Rose, what do you think?"

"I think I'm sorry that your man from Denver was killed and disposed of the way that he was. A decent person wouldn't do that to a dead dog, much less a human being. Custis, didn't you feel anything for the man?"

"Not much," Longarm said honestly. "Herb Pelkey was always threatening my boss with his Washington, D.C., connections. I didn't like or trust him, and neither did anyone else in our office."

"But to die and be tossed into a shitter like that, it's . . ."

Longarm pulled Rose close and kissed her cheek. "Listen," he told her. "In a few hours we are riding back to your ranch. The ranch that should be yours and *will* be yours. I don't know what's going to happen when we arrive. I hope that Andy is right when he says that we probably won't have to kill anyone, but you never know, so be prepared."

"And what happens after that?"

"I have no idea," Longarm said. "My guess is that within a week, Amos Ramsey will be back and he'll come at us with as many gunmen as he can find and hire. There will be a showdown, Rose. But we're going to pick the place, and it will be somewhere on your ranch, where we have the advantage . . . not them."

"I'll be thinking about that."

"Good. And now we still have some time. Do you want to try and get a little sleep?"

She hugged him tightly. "No, I want to make love."

Longarm was hoping for that answer. Hoping and already feeling himself rising to the occasion.

Chapter 23

It was half past midnight and the crescent moon was cradling a solitary star when Longarm, Rose, Sheriff Greer, and his deputy rode up to the Delamonte ranch fence line. There was a barbed wire gate entering the property, and now it hung wide open.

Rose looked at it and said, "I guess they're not worried about any cattle or horses running off the property. That means they've sold them all off or moved them onto their own big ranch."

"How many acres go with this ranch?" Longarm asked.

"Only about eighteen hundred, but we've got a good spring on the west side and a creek that runs most of the year."

"I've been out here a few times," Andy said. "This is one helluva nice ranch, Mrs. Delamonte."

"Thank you, Andy. My late husband and I intended to buy an English bull and upgrade our herd, but we were counting on making most of our profit on our ranch horses."

"You raised some fine horses," Lucas Greer said. "They still bring top dollar at every sale."

"It was our dream," Rose told them all, "and then Amos came and started to squeeze us to sell out. He kept increasing the pressure financially and by shooting our cattle when there was no one around, and when even that didn't work, he hired gunmen and left the rest up to his sons."

"How far ahead is the ranch house?" Longarm asked.

"It's just over that little hill," Rose said, riding through the open gate and on up the dirt track.

When they reached the top of the hill, there was just enough moon and starlight to see the dim outline of a ranch house, barns, and corrals, along with some big trees that gave the house shade. The stream that ran most of the year was a wavy line of silk laid against the backdrop of a jeweler's black velvet cloth. As far as Longarm could tell, the ranch rested in a cup with low mountains sloping into the valley from three sides.

"Beautiful setting even in poor light," he told Rose. "I can sure see why you want it back."

"I'd want it back if it was only a single acre of bad water and sage," she said, voice trembling with fury. "My husband and his parents are buried under those big trees and this was their home, and for a short while *my* home. It belongs to me, and I won't let a rich and hog-fat thief steal and then desecrate it with his bloody hands."

They all nodded without anything to say, until Longarm turned to Andy. "You say that there are a couple of cowboys living in the ranch house that are your friends?"

"They're sleeping in the bunkhouse," Andy said. "The cook and the head honcho named Burley are living in the house."

"And you're sure about that?"

"Yes, sir."

"All right," Longarm said, working it out in his mind. "What we'll do is ride around behind the bunkhouse, and Andy here can go inside and wake up the two cowboys. Andy, explain to them what we are going to do and that they'd better either side with us or just grab their clothes and start walking without making a sound."

"They're cowboys," Andy explained. "They ain't going to walk anyplace."

"Well," Longarm said, "they walk or they join us. That's the choice."

Sheriff Greer said, "I should ride up to the front of the house and announce myself. They'll either know me or know of me and come out. I can then give them the same option as you give the two cowboys."

Longarm considered that suggestion and then said, "Andy will sneak into the bunkhouse while you and I go up to the front of the house and call them outside."

"What am I supposed to do?" Rose asked.

"Just find a place in the trees and be ready to use that gun I gave you back in Denver," Longarm told her. "Hopefully, not a shot will be fired tonight."

"But . . ."

"Rose, I'm asking you to do this *my* way. The cook and this fella named Burley will recognize you, and that might push them into a fight. They won't recognize me, and I think we can do this peacefully."

"If we can't and they pull their guns," Rose told everyone, in a voice that brooked no room for debate, "I'll open fire."

"Rose," the sheriff told her, "I'm not sure if that would be such a good idea in this poor light. You might end up shooting the marshal and me by accident."

"I always hit what I aim for," Rose told the lawman. "Isn't that right, Custis?"

"It is for a fact," Longarm was forced to admit.

Sheriff Greer checked and then reholstered his gun. "All right. Andy, you go on up ahead and see if you can talk sense into your two cowboy friends."

"I'll do that," Andy promised.

"We'll give you five minutes," Longarm told the young Santa Fe deputy. "Then we're riding into the ranch yard."

They all nodded in agreement, and when Andy rode on down the hill toward the dark buildings, Sheriff Greer said, "He's got the makings of a fine lawman. I sure hope that there isn't a bad surprise awaiting Andy. I think the world of that kid."

"He's not a kid," Longarm countered. "He's your sworn deputy and he's wearing a badge. He's a man, and I've seen a whole lot younger than him in battle."

"You're talking about the war."

"I am," Longarm confessed. "I saw a lot of kids who hadn't even begun to shave fall on the battlefields. Your deputy will do just fine."

Sheriff Greer nodded, but even in the dark Longarm could see that he was very worried.

Fifteen minutes later, Andy and two skinny cowboys strolled out of the bunkhouse and joined Longarm and Sheriff Greer.

"I told you they had good sense," Andy whispered.

Sheriff Greer nodded. "You boys need to just get back behind the trees where you won't get shot if there is a battle. Mrs. Delamonte is out there, and she's going to cover us when we hail the ranch house."

"Burley might want to fight, but the old cook sure as hell won't," one of the cowboys said.

"Tell me about this Burley fella, but make it short."

"He's supposed to be from Montana," the cowboy said. "And I've seen him practice with a gun. He's fast and good. He's also a hard drinker and has a temper quicker than his trigger finger. He's the one to watch out for."

"He is," the other cowboy agreed. "I expect he's either drunk or hungover from drinking. He was pretty drunk at dinnertime."

"What's the cook's name?"

"Joe. He's a good man and a good cook."

"All right," Longarm said. "Now, you boys just start walking and don't stop until I holler out for you to come on back."

"Yes, sir."

Longarm looked at Andy. "Why don't you go along with your friends?"

"Don't insult me, Marshal Long. I know that I'm green and look more kid than man, but I've got sand in my craw and I wear a badge."

"Yes, you do," Longarm agreed. "All right. Cover your sheriff and myself when we go up to the house."

Longarm and Greer went right onto the porch, and they didn't knock but entered the dark house. "Burley, Joe! It's Sheriff Greer. You fellas get out of bed and come on out here into the front room. We all need to talk."

Longarm and the sheriff heard some swearing and the sound of a piece of furniture being knocked over. Finally, an old man in a dirty nightshirt appeared, blinking at the lamp that the sheriff had turned up.

"Sheriff Greer, what's . . . who's that with you?"

"This is Marshal Long. Where is Burley?"

"He's sleeping down the hall. He ain't going to like this any."

"I don't care. You step out to the porch and wait while we get Burley," Longarm ordered.

Joe hurried barefooted out onto the porch.

"Burley, get out here and keep your hands where I can see them," Greer shouted down the dim hallway.

The man named Burley shouted, "Go to hell, Greer!"

"Come on out or we're coming in!" Longarm bellowed.

Burley stuck his arm out of this bedroom door and fired two quick shots. Longarm fired back too late. Moments passed. They heard something and then gunshots in the yard.

"Oh, shit!" Greer cried. "Burley must have gone out the window and killed Andy!"

Longarm and Greer whirled and ran outside to see Andy standing over a naked and very dead man with a gun clenched in his fist.

Sheriff Greer dropped down on one knee and rolled the body over. "He has two bullet holes in the chest."

"He fired at me first," Andy swore. "I already had my gun in my hand and I just fired without even taking the time to aim. He looked like a ghost coming at me in the night."

"Well," Longarm said, "you did your duty and now he *is* a ghost."

Minutes later, Rose and the two cowboys were standing on the porch. Longarm said, "Joe, why don't you make us all up a big breakfast with lots of hot coffee. I don't think anyone will get any sleep tonight."

"Yes sir. I will do that. You ain't going to arrest me, are you, Sheriff?"

"Not if you make us a good breakfast," Sheriff Greer said with a straight face that caused everyone to laugh and break the tension.

"We can bury this fella Burley after daybreak," Long-arm said to no one in particular.

"Not near my in-laws or husband," Rose told him.

"Okay. Then where?"

"I got a place where they've buried the animals that have died on this ranch," Rose told him. "I remember where it is because at Christmas they butchered two hogs and buried the guts out yonder."

"You want Burley to be buried near hog guts?" Sheriff Greer asked.

"Sure do," Rose said, going into the house to help Joe with the breakfast.

Chapter 24

Five days later Sheriff Greer and Andy galloped into the ranch yard and yelled, "They're on their way!"

Longarm and Rose strode out to greet the pair, and when they were dismounted, Longarm asked, "When did Amos arrive back in Santa Fe?"

"He and Etta came in late last night. I didn't know until this morning when I went into the office."

"They might wait a few days to gather their forces," Longarm told everyone, including Joe and the two young cowboys.

"Not a chance of that happening," Rose told him. "I know Amos and Etta. They'll go to their own ranch and then they'll come straightaway to my ranch. Amos isn't going to wait one more hour than is necessary to wipe us out once and for all."

"Then we'd better get ready for a fight," Longarm said to everyone. "Sheriff Greer, are you and Andy with us or do you want to stay out of it and go back to town?"

"I'll stay," Andy said.

"We'll stay, too," one of the cowboys vowed.

But Sheriff Greer shook his head. "Andy, our job is in town. This ranch is out of our jurisdiction."

"Don't matter," Andy told his boss. "These folks are in the right and I intend to stay. You can fire me if you have to, but I'm not leavin'."

"I don't want to leave, either. But we're not hired to fight this battle."

"Then I quit," Andy said flatly.

"Damnation!" Greer swore. "I always counted on you to take my place when I retired."

"Thank you, but I'm obliged to quit anyway."

Longarm was proud of the young deputy and his cowboy friends. "Sheriff, you can ride on back and attend to your town duties. I won't hold it against you."

"No," Greer said after a long pause, "but *I'd* hold it against me. Rose, you've gotten a raw deal and now it's time for me to right a terrible wrong. So I guess that I'm staying."

"Don't 'guess' anything," Rose told him. "You've got a wife and family, so if you stand with us, you'd better stand tall and strong."

"I'll do that," Greer promised. "Amos Ramsey and his bunch should be along real soon. If they see me here, they might decide to back off from this fight so that no one dies."

"Don't count on it," Rose told the lawman. "You neither, Andy."

"No, ma'am."

Three tense hours later one of the cowboys was the first to spot the trail of dust in the sky. "Here they come!"

Longarm had laid a loose trap by assigning everyone

to a different shooting spot designed to surround the approaching force once they entered the ranch yard, while he, Rose, and Sheriff Greer would stand on the porch.

"Everyone to your places and get ready!" Longarm shouted.

Five minutes later, Amos Ramsey, sitting proudly in a fine carriage pulled by a big sorrel horse, stormed into the ranch yard flanked by four outriders. Etta was driving the carriage, and her eyes were wild with excitement as she hauled up on the reins.

When the carriage stopped and the dust settled, Longarm and Sheriff Greer stepped off the porch. "Amos, you and Etta are under arrest for the murders of the Delamonte family."

Amos barked a laugh. "Lucas, I'd heard that you crossed and went to the wrong side of the river. I didn't think you were that stupid, but I guess that I was wrong."

"Well, *I'm* not wrong anymore, Amos. You and Etta are under arrest."

"Got any proof against me or my daughter?"

"No, but I'm going to have after I interview all of your people. You can bet on that."

Amos shook his shaggy hair and glanced sideways at his beautiful daughter. "Etta," he said, "what do you think of that crock of shit?"

Etta smiled coldly. "I think that there are six of us and three of them."

"That's what I was thinking," Amos said. "We can settle this matter once and for all right now!"

Longarm saw the twin barrels of the hidden sawed-off shotgun come up from between Amos and Etta. He also saw in a heartbeat the four riders going for their weapons, and he barely had time to shout, "Open fire!"

What happened next passed in a red, deafening blur. Amos fired prematurely and took the head completely off the sorrel. Guns roared and riderless horses raced around and around in the confines of the ranch yard.

Etta Ramsey, screaming and badly wounded, fired at Rose Delamonte but missed. Rose aimed and drilled Etta through the forehead, slapping the once beautiful woman's head back against the seat cushion.

Longarm looked first to Rose. "Are you hit?"

"No," she told him. "Are you?"

"No."

Longarm glanced around and saw that Andy and Sheriff Greer were still standing without a scratch. The two cowboys came out from behind outbuildings, their eyes wide as they stared at the dead carriage horse and Ramsey cowboys, all of whom had been shot multiple times.

"Holy shit," Andy whispered. "I never thought I'd see anything like this."

"In all my days as a law officer, I've never seen anything to match this," Sheriff Greer said, holstering his empty pistol.

"I have," Longarm said, more to himself than to the others.

Rose walked slowly over to the bullet-riddled bodies. "I guess that's the end of it," she said. "They killed all of my family and now all of their family is gone, too."

"We'll see Judge Harper and have him set things right before he either resigns from the bench or goes straight to prison," Longarm promised.

Rose Delamonte nodded. "I hope they didn't sell off all my horses and cattle."

"I hope they didn't either," Longarm said. "But even if they did, you've still got one hell of a cache of gold to dig up."

Rose took him aside and they walked over to a cotton-wood tree. "You still want to be a part of this? We can dig the gold up and rebuild here as man and wife. You can see what a fine ranch this can become with a little work and some money. And I'll hire those two cowboys and Andy and . . ."

"Whoa," Longarm said, almost laughing as he pulled the woman close and held her tight. "You're moving way too fast for me, Rose."

She looked back at the ranch yard and all the death. "Life can be short and fast, Custis. I'm making you the offer of a lifetime."

He kissed her mouth. "Why don't we just sit on that offer for a few days? We've got Judge Harper to deal with and some things to sort out in town. Later on we can buy some champagne and dig up that hidden gold."

She turned her face up to his. "Custis, once we have it dug up, you wouldn't try and take advantage of me, would you?"

"Given the way you shoot, I'd be crazy to ever cross you, Rose."

She smiled, and tears filled her eyes. "We can make this work so well together. Will you at least *think* about my offer?"

"I'll think a lot about it," he admitted. "But right now I'm thinking about how nice it will be to make love to you again."

Rose shook her head in amazement. "You men! I offer you gold, my hand in marriage, and this ranch, and yet all you can think of is . . ."

"Yeah," Longarm admitted, "sometimes we're just plain hopeless and getting in bed with a beautiful woman like you is worth far more than gold."

Watch for

LONGARM AND THE CASTLE OF THE DAMNED

The 396th novel in the exciting LONGARM
series from Jove

Coming in November!

GIANT-SIZED ADVENTURE FROM AVENGING ANGEL LONGARM.

BY TABOR EVANS

penguin.com/actionwesterns